D1293593

DREAMS OF A DARK WARRIOR

"The richness of Cole's world and characters make it a fascinating place to visit!"

—*RT Book Reviews*

"Fast-paced, engaging, and captivating. . . . The perfect getaway."

—*Examiner.com*

DEMON FROM THE DARK

"Intense danger mixes with insatiable desire to create a scorching-hot romance that plays out against a fast-paced backdrop of thrilling supernatural adventure. Addictively good reading."

—*Love Vampires*

PLEASURE OF A DARK PRINCE

"There are few authors that can move me to tears. Kresley Cole is one of them."

—*Book Binge*

"Consistent excellence is a Cole standard!"

—*RT Book Reviews*

KISS OF A DEMON KING

"Cole deftly blends danger and desire into a brilliantly original contemporary paranormal romance . . . sexy romance . . . sharp humor . . . simply irresistible."

—*Reader to Reader*

DARK DESIRES AFTER DUSK

"Cole outdoes herself. . . . A gem."

—*RT Book Reviews*

BOOKS BY KRESLEY COLE

The Immortals After Dark Series

The Warlord Wants Forever
A Hunger Like No Other
No Rest for the Wicked
Wicked Deeds on a Winter's Night
Dark Needs at Night's Edge
Dark Desires After Dusk
Kiss of a Demon King
Deep Kiss of Winter
Pleasure of a Dark Prince
Demon from the Dark
Dreams of a Dark Warrior
Lothaire
Shadow's Claim
MacRieve
Dark Skye
Sweet Ruin
Shadow's Seduction
Wicked Abyss

The Game Maker Series

The Professional
The Master
The Player

The Arcana Chronicles

Poison Princess
Endless Knight
Dead of Winter
Day Zero
Arcana Rising

The MacCarrick Brothers Series

If You Dare
If You Desire
If You Deceive

The Sutherland Series

The Captain of All Pleasures
The Price of Pleasure

KRESLEY COLE

SHADOW'S SEDUCTION

VALKYRIE PRESS
New York • Dacia • Abaddon • Sylvan • New Orleans

VALKYRIE PRESS

Valkyrie Press
228 Park Ave S #11599
New York, NY 10003

ISBN 978-0-9972151-9-9
ISBN 978-0-9972151-8-2 (ebook)

Published in the United States of America.

Dear reader,

I'm so excited to share SHADOW'S SEDUCTION with you. Mirceo and Caspion's romance was a joy to write and came during a period when I dearly needed a manuscript to play nice with me! This probably had to do with the fact that I've been noodling their love story for years, even before they became Mirceo and Caspion.

I could argue that I've been waiting to pen their tale since I read my first modern male-male romance novel back in 1996. Twenty years—and many happily-ever-afters—later, I finally got to. . . .

The Lore

"... and those sentient creatures that are not human shall be united in one stratum, coexisting with, yet secret from, man's."

- Most are immortal, able to regenerate from injuries.

- Their eyes change to a breed-specific color with intense emotion.

The Vampires

- Each adult male vampire walks as the living dead until he finds his mate, a fated one who will render his body fully alive, giving him breath and making his heart beat, a process known as *blooding*.

- If a vampire drinks blood directly from the flesh, he can harvest his victim's memories. Biting too many or drinking a victim to death can make a vampire grow red-eyed and crazed, a condition known as *bloodlust*.

- *Tracing* is teleporting. A vampire can only trace to destinations he's previously been.

- Three vampire factions exist: the Forbearer Army (turned humans), the Horde (red-eyed flesh-takers), and the Dacians (thought to be mythical)....

The Dacians

"Whispered to have vast intellects and stony hearts, the vampires of mist and legend observe the Lore with dispassionate eyes. Cursed with unending strife until the House of Old rises. . . ."

- Dacia's closed kingdom, the Realm of Blood and Mist, is said to be hidden within a hollowed-out mountain range.

- They are stronger and faster than other vampires, with esoteric abilities.

The Demonarchies

"The demons are as varied as the bands of man. . . ."

- A collection of demon dynasties.

- Most demon breeds can teleport to places they've previously been.

The Death Demons

"Violent, warlike, and ruthless, they constantly hunger for their next kill—and the power it brings. . . ."

- A demonarchy located in the remote plane of Abaddon.

- They harvest physical strength with each kill they make.

The Accession

"And a time shall come to pass when all immortal beings in the Lore must fight and destroy each other."

- A kind of mystical checks-and-balances system for an ever-growing population of immortals.

- Occurs every five hundred years. Or right now . . .

SHADOW'S
SEDUCTION

Life is merely a game I was born to win.
—MIRCEO DACIANO, PRINCE OF DACIA,
LAST MALE SCION OF THE HOUSE OF CASTELLAN

When I was young, I had no choice but to beg for food. Choices can only be appreciated by those who've had none.
—CASPION THE TRACKER, BOUNTY HUNTER,
PARENTAGE UNKNOWN

ONE

I like your style, demon."

Cas had just tipped his head back to relax in the warm springs when he heard that low voice above all the others in the bathhouse.

He sat upright on the underwater bench and gazed over in that direction, peering through the steam across the sizable pool. Hooded gray eyes stared back at him.

The black-haired vampire? The ladies at this palace whispered that he was a prince of some ancient line, rich beyond measure, and a generous lover of both males and females. He was a contradiction—a natural-born vampire whose eyes were clear of the red that signaled bloodlust.

Fawning admirers surrounded the prince; so why would he be addressing Cas?

"My style?" *He must've watched me tonight.* Cas was fresh from the Monday night free-for-all, an orgy with hundreds of immortals. He'd just stopped for a soak and a last mug of cheap brew before returning to his home realm of Abaddon.

To face his failure. The first-ever hunt he couldn't complete.

The vampire's expression was amused. "I saw you in action earlier, sweetheart."

Cas's face warmed at that endearment. Blushing? As a demon well-versed in sex, he didn't *blush*. "We do what we can."

The prince laughed, the rich sound pleasing to the ear. A lock of shoulder-length black hair fell over one of those gray eyes, and he smoothed it back. Though his clean-shaven face was vampire pale, his high cheekbones were tinged with healthy color. "A charmer, aren't you?" He had a thick accent. Romanian? "Come join us."

Everyone in the bathhouse—immortals fucking on lounge chairs, in the water, even in the air—seemed to be watching this exchange.

What does he want with me? "I'm good, thanks."

Gasps sounded from all around. The prince's brows shot up with surprise. *Never been turned down before?* With a slow grin spreading over his face, the vampire rose and began making his way across the pool.

Those deserted admirers shot Cas killing looks. As if he'd sought this attention? He was straight, which the prince would have gathered if he'd truly watched Cas *in action*.

Instead of tracing, the vampire chose to wade through the waist-deep water. He looked to be a few inches shorter than Cas's seven feet. Whereas Cas possessed a brawny build, the prince was leanly muscled.

Other immortals clocked his hypnotic movements. A succubus riding a blue zalos demon on a massage table tweaked her nipples as she stared. When the prince passed a nymph—who was getting railed from behind by a huffing warlock—she stretched just to brush her fingertips along his arm.

Typical vampire magnetism. In order to feed, members of that species lured other beings within striking range. A biological necessity made vampires some of the most mesmerizing creatures in the Lore.

Once he reached Cas, the prince stretched out on the narrow bench beside him, utterly at ease. "Greetings, demon."

Cas inclined his head. "What's brought you over here?" *Into this darkened corner. With me.*

"My cock." The vampire gestured to his semihard shaft, visible through the steam and water.

Cas tensed. "Pardon?"

"The wayward thing has a mind of its own. It points, and I must follow." Staring down, he gave a woebegone sigh. "If only it weren't so beautiful . . ."

"Your wayward cock was mistaken to point you in my direction." *A sentence I never thought I'd say.* Already in this limited exchange, Cas had lost his equilibrium and couldn't quite recover it.

The prince raised his gaze. "I'm jesting with you," he said, immediately mouthing, *I'm not jesting with you.*

"I desire only females, friend."

The vampire's lips curved, revealing white teeth and fangs. "My own desires are not as . . . restricted. But I have others who can sate those needs. I didn't seek you out for a mere fuck."

He didn't want to fuck Cas? An odd thought arose: *What does he find objectionable about me?* "Then what do you want?"

"For now, I'll have your name."

He grudgingly answered, "Caspion." The other males Cas hung out with—rowdy demons in Abaddon and fellow bounty hunters—seemed far less *complex* than this vampire.

"I'm Prince Mirceo. Call me Mirceo."

"Prince of what kingdom?"

"A secret one. I'm afraid I can't tell you more."

Was this vampire toying with him? Though Cas's closest friend, Bettina, was heir to the throne of their demonarchy, he mistrusted the wealthy. Bettina was the rare exception.

Mirceo said, "Already I break the laws of my people, just by conversing with an otherlander."

Cas doubted the prince wanted only conversation. *They always want more.* He felt as if he lived two lives: his normal existence in Abaddon, and his shadow life filled with sexual exploits. No one in his shadow life cared to *converse* with a demon like Cas. "You joined me for a reason. . . ."

"Perhaps I seek the friendship of a fellow erotic connoisseur. Tell me about yourself."

Why waste his time with me? Unlike the others here, Cas had little money and zero education. He'd grown up on the streets, wearing rags, scavenging from refuse bins, and begging. He'd had no name, so everyone had called him *Beggar.*

Cas came to this opulent pleasure den solely because the management let him in for free, and the women were always stunning.

The vampire must still think he had a shot at sex. The two of them sat unclothed on a bench that seemed to shrink by the instant. If Cas moved his leg by even an inch, his bare thigh would brush the vampire's. "I meant what I said, prince. I appreciate your interest, but I don't return it."

"My interest at present is in your mind, Caspion. I've a vampire's curiosity, and your behavior fascinates me. Answer a few of my questions, and share some drink with me." He waved for one of the servers.

"My *mind?*" Cas couldn't keep the disbelief out of his voice.

All but illiterate, he could only read the words most commonly used on bounty postings.

"Yes, your mind."

Flattered, Cas sat a little taller.

The server arrived, a shapely demoness who cast Mirceo a look of longing. Had the vampire enjoyed that beauty? According to others, he'd been with most here—because he refused to repeat bedmates.

Mirceo ordered blood mead for himself and the palace's best demon brew for his "handsome new friend."

Cas raised his brows at the vintage, one he'd never been able to afford. Like most demons, he loved brew. "Perhaps I could remain for a round." He didn't want to return to home yet anyway. He was weary to his bones, had come to this place to release tension.

"Good choice." Mirceo flashed him a smile of praise. "Ah, sweetheart, what fun you and I shall have together."

For some reason, a shiver crossed Cas's nape. The vampire's words were harmless enough. *So why do I feel like I just agreed to far more than a drink?*

TWO

Be a lamb and keep the drinks coming," Mirceo told the server when she returned with two golden chalices. She was a storm demoness who'd delivered a memorable blowjob the other night.

Her eyes begged for a repeat. His eyes said, *My apologies, tulip, but it will not happen.*

A devoted hedonist, Mirceo had few hard and fast rules in his life—but he never revisited partners.

Once she left, Caspion took a swig from his chalice, then licked his lips. "By all the gods, that's smooth. It must cost a fortune."

I would spend a true fortune just to see you lick those lips again. "I'm a vampire with more gold than time," he said absently, his gaze roaming over Caspion's flawless features— midnight-blue eyes, chiseled chin and jawline, a mouth made for kissing.

And those horns! They curved back along his fair head like a crown of polished amber, the perfect complement to his careless blond hair and sun-kissed skin.

The demon's towering body exuded sex and power, the most magnificent Mirceo had ever beheld.

Well, outside of his own glorious form. *I want him.*

Earlier in the orgy, Mirceo had been pile-driving his third partner—a delightfully greedy succubus—when he'd spotted the demon. "Who's the blond?" The way that male had pleasured—and controlled—his own partner was spellbinding.

Between panting breaths, the succubus had said, "Caspion the Tracker . . . a death demon."

A little later, one of Mirceo's hedonist friends had noticed his gaze drawn repeatedly to the demon, saying, "He's a favorite of the ladies. Let's put it this way: he's the sole male here who doesn't have to pay admission."

"Is he a favorite of any gents?"

"Inflexibly hetero."

"Is he, then?" Mirceo had smiled. "I like a challenge. He'll become the conquest of conquests." His friends had laid wagers. Amazingly, some were foolish enough to bet against Mirceo Daciano. . . .

Now he raised his chalice to the demon. "Shall we have a toast?"

Caspion raised his own. "What should we drink to?"

"Why, to the bottom, of course."

They downed their cups, and the demoness was quick with the refills.

Once she'd left again, Caspion said, "I've accepted your payment, vampire. Ask your questions."

Tonight this deliciously dominant male had given Mirceo two things no one else here would dare: a refusal and an order. Mirceo found his lack of deference . . . thrilling. "Straight down to business, then? Am I such loathsome company that you can't wait to get out of my clutches?" *I need to clutch those bronzed pecs. While nuzzling the golden chest hair between them.* "Very well, demon, I want to know what you were thinking about in that orgy. You certainly didn't have your mind on your partners."

Tension stole over his broad shoulders. "I heard no complaints."

Sensitive, sweetheart? "Indeed not. That's part of my interest. Though your thoughts were a million leagues away, you wrung orgasms from those females like juice from grapes." He'd been all-alpha, calling the shots—as Mirceo himself always did.

"Sometimes my mind wanders during sex." When Caspion rubbed his nape, Mirceo's attention flicked from the demon's bulging bicep to the sexy blond hair of his armpit. "How long were you watching me?"

"Long enough to grow intrigued." Mirceo met his gaze. "I must know what you were contemplating."

"I'm not used to revealing private details to strangers." He took a generous swig of his drink, blue eyes growing stormy.

Gods, those eyes. *I want to look up into them as I take his shaft between my lips.* Mirceo stilled at the thought. He'd never been the one on his knees—he was a prince, after all—but he might sample a cock if it belonged to Caspion. *Perhaps I should get pointers from the demoness server?* "Shall I go first?" he asked. "Will you trust me if I tell you details from my own life?"

"Depends on what you share."

"Very well." Lowering his tone—one of Mirceo's most fool-proof seduction weapons was his raspy, accented voice—he murmured, "I come from a fabled realm that few outsiders have ever seen." *Hidden within a mountain, the kingdom of Dacia spreads beneath a soaring cavern.* "Considered a vampire's paradise, it's filled with riches." *Blood runs in fountains, fog wisps over cobblestone streets, and a giant diamond in the highest part of the cavern*

filters the sun. "My kind have abilities that other vampires do not."
We can turn into mist and levitate. "I'm forbidden to leave my
kingdom without the permission of a gatekeeper—yet I do leave,
often." *Because the gatekeeper likes his blood mead a little too well.*
"Though I'm to stay hidden in mist, unseen by anyone outside of
our realm—I am seen by others, regularly."

If one departed Dacia without permission, he could never
trace home, and memories of the kingdom's location would fade.
But I found ways around that.

The demon's lids were half-masted. He looked as if he could
have listened to Mirceo speak for eternity. "Is your father the king?"

"We have no king at present." Even over the smells of hot
springs and sex, Mirceo caught a thread of Caspion's natural
scent—a heady blend that called to mind raindrops and leather.
As one who hailed from a realm with no rain, Mirceo found the
demon's scent as exotic as it was tantalizing.

Caspion took a deep drink. "If you're a prince, why haven't
you taken the throne?"

"Others in my family have as much claim as I. The situation
is fraught. There's another who could rule us—the rightful heir."
Lothaire the Enemy of Old, a three-thousand-year-old vampire.
"But his eyes are red." He was half Horde, half Dacian.

"From bloodlust."

"Indeed." Mirceo sipped his chalice. "He's crazed with it. In
my particular kingdom, drinking from the flesh is considered
a heinous taboo. Naturally I fantasize about it without cease."
Caspion's pulse point drew his gaze, and the demon noticed, swal-
lowing thickly. "My relatives and I have agreed to think on the
matter and decide soon." Mirceo would vote to install Lothaire
without hesitation. Nothing could shatter Dacia's blood-taking
taboo like a red-eyed king. "Are you satisfied with my details?"

Caspion nodded. His drink seemed to be hitting him. He must be unused to the potency of expensive vintages. "My oldest friend—a Sorceri/demon halfling—was assaulted by a gang of Vrekeners." Eyes flickering black with emotion, he said, "The attack was more vicious than anything I've ever seen; she barely survived. For sixty days, I sat at her bedside while she recovered. For sixty nights, I set out into the worlds to hunt her assailants."

She sounds like more than a friend. "I'm a bounty hunter by trade, but those winged fiends are hidden from me, their floating lair constantly moving. Today I was ordered off the search."

"I'm sorry, Caspion. That must be difficult to accept. If I can be of service, tell me."

"Why?" The demon grew cagey. "You don't know me."

True. "I can't explain it, but I feel an affinity with you." Perhaps he would remain friends with Caspion, even after they'd partaken of each other. *There's a first time for everything.* "It is unusual." Being near this male made him feel at once stimulated and satisfied. Enlivened, yet soothed.

"Unusual? You're a favorite here. Everyone vies for your attention. I'd say you feel *an affinity* with many."

Mirceo slid him a grin. "So you've noticed me?"

Caspion scowled into his cup.

"My home, though a paradise, is full of rules, so I enjoy other-landers' company. But none so much as yours." Not a lie.

"I doubt that," the demon said, revealing another intriguing facet to his personality: insecurity. This mighty blond Adonis was vulnerable. It made Mirceo want to champion him, to clutch him close.

Protectiveness? How unlike me. He only ever felt protective of Kosmina, his cherished younger sister. The rest of the beings in the worlds could all go to hell as far as he was concerned.

"Why should I believe anything you say?" Caspion asked.

"Why *shouldn't* you? Also, do recall that a natural-born vampire like myself is incapable of lying." Mirceo studied the demon's breathtaking face. "Do you not feel a like affinity with me?"

~

Weirdly, Cas did. Or maybe he was enjoying the effects of the smoothest—yet strongest—brew he'd ever consumed. After all, why would he feel a connection with a sophisticated vampire prince? "Not a sexual affinity, though."

Mirceo ran his fingers along the rim of his chalice, his black claws trimmed shorter than Cas's own. "So you've never been with a male."

He shook his head. "Not my cup of tea."

"It wasn't mine either, until I had a sip." Mirceo took a drink, then licked a drop of blood mead from his lip.

The sight held Cas rapt before he blinked back to attention. How to respond to that comment? *I see. Very good. Thanks for sharing.*

"So what shall we do about your hunt?" the vampire asked, mercifully moving to another subject.

"There's nothing I *can* do. I must follow my order." Raum, one of Bettina's guardians and the acting ruler of Abaddon, had vowed to send a cadre of his finest warriors to take over. "I find myself . . . adrift."

"Is this female you sought to avenge more than a friend?"

"Though she's beautiful and talented—she's a goldsmith without equal—I'll never view her as more than a sister." Cas had taken her to the mortal realm to explore, teaching her what baseball was and how to drive a car.

But lately, his visits with her had grown increasingly awkward. She was ashamed of how she'd reacted to her gruesome injuries, wishing she'd been more *demonic*. Stronger. Yet the delicate halfling had never looked or acted as if she had demon blood. "I've known her for more than a decade, ever since I was fifteen."

"You're twenty-five? Five years younger than me. Are you fully immortal?"

"Just transitioned." Little other than decapitation could kill Cas now.

"Regrettably, I'm right behind you. My heart has been slowing for years, soon to stop beating." With his transition, a male vampire would go into a kind of walking stasis—heartbeat, respiration, and sexual ability dormant—only to be awakened by his vampire Bride. "Listen." Mirceo held up a hand to pause the conversation for several moments, then pointed at his chest. "My heart was motionless for that entire time. I figure I have another couple of months before I can no longer fuck—until I find *my mate*," he added darkly. "The prospect of a walking-dead existence is unfortunate enough, but to depend on a stranger to revive me? And then she'll expect me to be faithful to her." He shuddered. "So my upside is one partner. Forever."

"Gods, I feel for you about the celibacy, friend." These days, sex seemed to be the only thing keeping Cas sane. The problem was money. Cas didn't get free admission at every establishment.

The life of a player was an impoverished one. Not to mention the sums he spent to fund apprenticeships for pups in Abaddon.

"You don't sympathize about the monogamy? I consider it an intolerable hardship."

"Once I find my female, I'll be loyal to my dying breath." Though Cas was young, he already longed for her and the younglings she'd give him.

"At least you can keep fucking until then. No end in sight for *your* cockstands."

Cas countered, "At least you know what it's like to spill seed." A male demon could orgasm before he claimed his fated one, but he couldn't release semen until he lost his demon seal inside his mate's body. "Why are you so against monogamy?"

"My predatory nature makes me forever pursue new conquests. Would you track prey you'd already captured? Would a hunter stalk a boar he'd already felled?" Mirceo sighed. "Once my heart stops, it won't matter anyway. But until then, I intend to fuck like a madman, sampling every wicked delight available to a vampire with more gold than time and less wisdom than daring."

Must be nice.

"Join me, sweetheart. My treat. We'll journey the worlds, sharing wenches and drink. I'll take you to bacchanalia that will make tonight's affair appear tame. I'll introduce you to gods, and we'll wallow in meaningless hedonism."

After Cas's last two months, that sounded so bloody tempting. If the spoiled prince wanted to pay, maybe Cas should simply enjoy. But first he'd get one thing clear. . . . "If you think to seduce me, it won't happen. I will never desire another male."

Holding Cas's gaze, he said, "Around me, you won't ever do anything you don't wish." The vampire leaned in closer. "Isn't that the essence of hedonism? Partaking of all the things you *want* and none of the things you *don't*?"

Cas couldn't seem to look away. Up this close, he spied a ring of black encircling Mirceo's irises. *Mesmerizing . . .* "So why me? Any number of these beings would leap at the offer you just made."

The vampire's lips curved. "What you do with a partner's body can only be considered art. Young demon, consider me a patron of the arts. . . ."

THREE

"O ur time grows nigh, Caspion," the prince told him in a grave tone.

He and Cas sat atop the tower of a suspension bridge in the mortal world. Hundreds of feet above the water, they gazed out at the shroud of fog. As usual, they each had a flask.

"But it's only been a few weeks." As promised, the vampire had opened Cas's eyes to a dazzling new world, taking him everywhere from erotic balls to sordid dungeons, while plying him with the finest delicacies and drink. "What's the rush?"

They'd packed three months of living into these three weeks, rarely sleeping, becoming inseparable. They matched appetites and predilections—for the most part, at least. Mirceo would bed a male as readily as a female. Had no preference.

Cas pointed out, "Your heart's still beating." Occasionally. "There are still pleasures to be had." Even nonsexual ones.

After nights spent fighting drunken brawls and plowing earthy courtesans, Cas and Mirceo talked into the day, telling each other secrets. . . .

Mirceo: *"I'm a Dacian. I come from the hidden Realm of Blood and Mist."* Supposedly an actual myth, Dacians were said to be stronger, faster, and more ruthless than other vampires. *"I'm the head of the castle guard, but I've little responsibility because the black-stone fortress lies empty without a king."*

Cas: *"I was a street orphan with no idea who my parents were."* Shame had prevented him from revealing his past as a lowly beggar, but he'd admitted, *"Though I taught myself to read basic words from bounty postings, I've never even attempted a book."*

After that, the vampire had begun reading to him each morning. Cas enjoyed those soothing lulls far more than the revelry. . . .

Now the prince sighed. "I miss my sister and my home. Plus there is the matter of crowning a new king."

The crazed one? Gods help them.

Mirceo peered at Cas. "Will you miss me when I go?" The vampire's gray eyes matched the fog ghosting over the water. Like that mist, Mirceo had seeped under Cas's skin, into his very bones.

"You know I will." Cas was happier than he'd ever been. Despite their fundamental differences, their personalities had meshed in an effortless ebb and flow. "My instincts are telling me to keep you close."

Only one thing marred their time together. He wished Mirceo would quit using his seductive powers on him. All vampires possessed that supernatural allure, but Mirceo's was nearly irresistible. Their bond needed no such distraction.

Mirceo turned to take in the surreal scene. "I have a theory as to why we feel so connected."

So did Cas. He believed fate had given him the foundation for what would become a legendary friendship—in order to make up for all the things Cas had lacked: parents, a home, *food*. His earliest memory was of clutching his stomach against hunger pangs. "Tell me your theory."

"You know how much I adore my little sister?"

"Yes." The vampire often spoke of her. After their parents had been murdered by another royal, Mirceo had become Mina's entire world, and she his.

Facing him again, Mirceo said, "Caspion, I believe you might be . . . her mate."

Cas's breath left him. That would mean Mirceo was his brother-by-fate. *Of course!*

~

Mirceo didn't think *anyone* could deserve his beloved sister—he'd raised her since she was a bashful, six-year-old imp—but Caspion came closest.

"A fated connection to your family?" Excitement lit the demon's expression. "Finally something to explain our connection."

"Where nothing else could?" Mirceo murmured. As a prince of Dacia, he'd never had a best friend. *I'd hoped that I might have something to do with this bond.*

"That came out wrong." Caspion took a drink from his flask. "I only meant that we have so many differences—our species, backgrounds, occupations, and . . . stations. We don't have much that ties us together."

But we finish each other's sentences. Our minds seem to be synced. We trust one another.

Did his affection for Caspion run deeper than the reverse? How? Mirceo was beloved by everyone, celebrated in his kingdom. And in his otherland social circle. And in pleasure palaces the Lore over. "In any case, Mina is of age now." Females grew into full immortality earlier than males—with no *blooding* drama to deal with. Mina had transitioned a few months ago, right around the time she'd turned twenty-one.

He pulled out a picture of her that he always kept in his pocket. Handing it to Caspion, he said, "May I present Princess Kosmina." In the likeness, fair Mina gave a shy smile.

"Stunning." The demon's pupils enlarged at the sight. "But I never saw myself with a royal. Someone so superior." Caspion cared more about class distinctions than anyone Mirceo had ever known—yet he never fawned or groveled.

"Being considered *superior* would amuse her. She's deathly shy and passive, can't meet a stranger's eyes."

"A passive female would suit me well."

Hard to believe that not even a month ago, Mirceo had planned to bed this demon and win a wager. *The joke's on me.* Caspion, his possible brother-by-fate, was officially *off* the menu.

Pity. Mirceo had begun to suspect he could truly seduce Caspion, dragging him over the finish line. Though the demon had shown no desire to join in when Mirceo bedded males, he'd never seemed particularly averse to it either. "Basically, she's as retiring as I am arrogant—except when she's sword fighting. Mina is a mistress at arms."

"She sounds incredible." Caspion gazed over at Mirceo with an unsure expression. "How would you feel about a no-name demon paired with your beloved sister?"

Rolling his eyes, Mirceo shoved him off the bridge.

Used to Mirceo's antics, the demon simply traced back into place. Attention on the likeness, Caspion said, "I do feel something for her. A sense." He flashed Mirceo his heartbreakingly boyish smile. "You help me with your sister, and we'll give you a score of nieces and nephews." The demon had told Mirceo he wanted dozens of children, reasoning: *Though I have no line before me, I could forgive fate for that if I had a line to come after me.* "When can I meet her?"

"There's the catch. It's too dangerous for her to leave Dacia." A plague in the otherlands had wiped out female vampires, even fully immortal ones. "And we allow no passing visitors inside our hidden realm. You'll be denied entry—unless you're willing to remain in our underworld forever."

"I'd be trapped down there?"

"Worse. You *can* leave, but if you did, you'd be hunted by my uncle Trehan." Mina and Mirceo were so young compared to their older cousins that they called Trehan, Viktor, and Stelian *uncle.* "You would leave only to die."

"I can't meet her for five minutes just outside of your realm?"

Mirceo took the portrait back. "Though she would love to venture forth, I will *never* permit it." He shuddered at the thought of losing her.

"Then what choice do I have?" Caspion said. "Something is at work here. My instincts tell me to go, and I trust them." He squared his shoulders. "I'm prepared to take this risk."

"I want you to think about your decision overnight."

Surprise flickered over the demon's face. "What's to think about? What male wouldn't rush headlong to meet his beautiful mate?"

"Hear me, friend"—Mirceo pinned Caspion's gaze with his own—"your choice will affect the rest of your eternal life."

FOUR

The Realm of Blood and Mist

*T*he demon is officially back on the menu.

"I have a surprise for you," Mirceo said at the end of Caspion's first week in Dacia. They stood on the balcony of Mirceo's sprawling clifftop villa, one nearly as elevated as the empty royal castle.

As he and Caspion surveyed the sleepy realm and drank from crystal chalices, Mirceo savored the demon's rain-and-leather scent. *Everything I can do not to bite him . . .*

"A surprise?" Caspion asked absently, taking a drink. Since discovering he felt nothing more than brotherly affection for Mina, he'd been rocked with disappointment. He'd confessed to feeling protective of her—much as he did with Bettina.

But Mina's loss was her brother's gain. Mirceo had become convinced he could bed the demon. Over the last week, he could swear Caspion's regard for him had deepened. Little hints made Mirceo hope.

A glimmer of awareness in the demon's eyes. An overlong stare. A change in his scent.

Whenever Caspion grew lusty, his rain-and-leather thread skewed more toward leather; Mirceo had picked up on that—when the two of them had been alone together.

Yet he was running out of time—his heart continued to slow—which meant he could no longer play fair with the demon. *Tonight it will happen.* "Yes, a particularly toothsome surprise."

In a noncommittal tone, Caspion said, "Your surprises always are." He seemed even less interested in the debauchery they'd enjoyed.

Mirceo's interest had waned as well. He'd used to love watching Caspion in the throes with others, but lately he'd experienced only dissatisfaction. He asked the demon, "What's going on in that head of yours?" Mirceo's ever-growing lust was equaled only by his fascination with Caspion's mind.

What shadows lurked? What hidden desires lay untapped? He found himself hanging on this male's every word.

Unhappiness tinged Caspion's eyes. "This place is a marvel, and I'm one of the few outsiders who's seen it. Not bad for a no-name demon." When Caspion had first beheld Mirceo's lavish residence, he'd pulled at his collar, fearing he'd break something valuable.

So Mirceo had set about smashing priceless vases until Caspion had cast him a hint of that boyish grin. Later, the demon had stared in awe at Mirceo's book collection. Though Caspion had never been jealous of his wealth, a stark envy had burned in the demon's eyes when he'd asked, "You've read all of those?"

Mirceo had already been planning to teach him to read. "I have," he'd answered. "And I promise you, my brilliant friend, you will as well. . . ."

Now Mirceo canted his head. "You didn't eat much at dinner."

Caspion had been surprised by the extravagant delicacies available in the kingdom, until he'd seen the number of otherlanders who made permanent homes here. Plus, vampire young ate food of the earth. He shrugged. "After so many years of hunger, I never thought I could lack an appetite."

Mirceo couldn't imagine starving. As perilous as royal life could be in Dacia, he and Mina had wanted for nothing.

Caspion's discontent was weighing on him, much as his sister's would. A crazy idea crossed his mind. *What if the demon is* my *mate?* Same-sex pairings weren't unheard of.

Mirceo couldn't know until his heart went full-stop. If it then restarted . . . "Do you have any theories about our strong affinity now?"

Caspion leaned against the balcony railing. "There are tales that have been passed down through generations of legendary friendships. Balladeers sing songs about them. I believe you and I share such a friendship."

In a softer tone, Mirceo said, "Yes. I like that idea." It made more sense than his own far-fetched notion. What hope did a thirty-year-old vampire have of finding his mate? "But you're not happy here?"

Caspion hiked his broad shoulders. "I took a chance. Given the same information, I would take that risk again."

"That's not what I asked."

"My instincts drew me to this place." The demon trusted his instincts more than Mirceo managed to do with his own. "But I do regret not checking on Bettina first. Coming here was rash. I got so caught up, so tunnel-visioned toward a certain future, that I couldn't see the things that are most important to me."

Mirceo wanted to be the most important thing to him. *Damn it, why does he not fawn over me as others always do?*

Caspion continued, "She is still vulnerable, and now I can't protect her." Without the ability to turn to mist, the demon wouldn't get permission to exit the kingdom. "She's used to me going away on jobs for months at a time, but things had been in flux when I left."

"What do you mean?"

"There was talk of going back to olden demonic ways." At Mirceo's questioning look, Caspion explained, "Marrying her off to whichever suitor is strongest."

"Surely she wouldn't agree to such a barbaric plan."

Caspion said, "Her guardians can be persuasive."

"Then I can go and watch over her. I'll check on her regularly."

Frustration thinned the demon's lips. "That's not the same." Caspion was as loyal as a Lykae.

"We'll figure something out. . . ." Mirceo trailed off when feminine laughter sounded from inside the villa. "For now let's enjoy the present. Our entertainment has arrived."

~

The night's becoming a blur.

Mirceo's surprise was a trio of ravishing nymphs—a pale redhead, an olive-skinned brunette, and a curvaceous blonde—who made their home in Dacia. After flirting, teasing, and drinking, the five had ended up on Mirceo's mammoth bed.

But Cas's mind was wandering. He hadn't resigned himself to never seeing the outside world again. *Just don't do anything rash until then, Tina.*

Not as Cas had done. Yes, he'd taken a night to contemplate his decision to come here, but he'd spent it imagining a future with Kosmina. . . .

Mirceo's banter with one of the nymphs roused him from his thoughts. As usual, the prince had focused his attentions on a redhead. When Mirceo laughed at the female's playful teasing, Cas grew distracted, scarcely noticing as the other two removed their tops.

For weeks, Cas had watched Mirceo bed any available beauty—they'd even shared females—but Mirceo's enjoyment of that redhead irritated Cas for some reason.

Like claws down a chalkboard. Was it because Cas had drunk too much tonight?

The prince caught him frowning, so Cas averted his gaze, reaching for the busty brunette to knead a plump breast. That delight should have filled his shaft with blood, but he . . . flagged. She even stroked his horns—which demons loved. So why did he wish this night was already over? As he dropped his hand, he found Mirceo's attention on him.

The air between them seemed taut. Awareness prickled. Why had Mirceo's addictive scent—sandalwood with a hint of blood—never registered with him before? Why had Cas never noticed the heat his vampiric body gave off?

The redhead noticed them staring at each other. "You two should kiss."

With a smile in his tone, Mirceo said, "What an intriguing idea, tulip." The vampire traced to sit beside him at the foot of the bed.

"Hardly," Cas said. "I only pleasure females."

The brunette stood, crossing her arms over her chest. "Nothing would *pleasure* us more than seeing you two masculine specimens lock lips."

The blonde stood as well, leaving Cas and Mirceo on the bed. She joined the other two—nymphs in solidarity.

Mirceo laughed again, treating Cas to that rich, throaty sound. "It's just a lark, sweetheart. Something to titillate our ladies. I can scent them growing wet in anticipation."

The redhead said, "Perhaps the demon hunter isn't as secure in his tastes as we thought."

Cas raised his brows. "I'm very secure." He knew two things about his sexuality. *I've always been attracted to females, and I've never been attracted to males.* So why did Mirceo's vampire charisma seem to get stronger every day?

Maybe Cas *should* press his lips to Mirceo's—to cure himself of this growing obsession with the prince.

Clasping her hands in front of her chest, the redhead said, *"Pleeeeease.* Something to remember for the rest of our eternal lives."

Cas turned toward Mirceo to crack a joke. "I've done a lot of things to get laid, but—"

The vampire's mouth met his.

Sensation flooded Cas, electricity crackling up and down his spine. *Too much, too . . .* He tensed to jerk away, but Mirceo darted his tongue between Cas's parted lips.

Fuuuck. Their tongues touched. Cas's head swam.

Stop. What the hell are you doing? STOP.

The vampire threaded his fingers through Cas's hair to draw him even closer. Breaking away from Mirceo's carnal mouth felt impossible. Some kind of madness was overtaking him! He found himself . . . giving a tentative flick of his pointed tongue. Then another. *Why can't I stop?*

The prince submitted, letting him delve. *Tasting Mirceo. Exploring this.* The vampire's lips yielded beneath his own.

Curiosity goaded Cas to take another lick. A nip. One more taste, then he'd end this. One more dip into this unfamiliar well.

Yet soon raw lust overwhelmed curiosity. He slanted his mouth over the vampire's, demanding more. Their tongues twined, their breaths gone ragged. *My gods, this feels so fucking good.*

Dimly, Cas realized the giggling females were closing the bedroom door behind them.

He roused, his mind struggling to come back online. Mirceo's moan slammed him right back into this kiss.

Just one last taste. . . .

FIVE

C as collapsed at the vampire's side. They lay sprawled on the bed, heaving breaths, both still dressed.

Cas threw an arm over his face. *What the hell just happened?* Sweat coated his body. Shock consumed him.

He shifted his arm to glance at Mirceo. When the prince stretched with a smug grin and a sound of satisfaction, one word blasted through Cas's head.

ESCAPE.

He shot upright. *I just got off with Mirceo.*

The prince's smile faded. "This isn't so monumental a thing, Caspion. Just a lark. Just pleasure." Of course it was *just pleasure* to him.

While Cas felt scalded and exposed—as if his entire body were a new wound—Mirceo remained unchanged, offering nothing else of himself.

"We still have our pants on." With a hint of amusement in his eyes, the vampire said, "Though mine *are* filled with semen."

The intoxicating scent of it made Cas' cock stir for more. What godsdamned power did Mirceo wield over him?

Whatever the vampire saw in his expression made him sit up. "Be at ease, friend."

"At ease?" Cas had never felt more lust for another. How had he gone from desiring only females to desiring Mirceo? *Wait . . .* Cas's eyes narrowed. "You fucking mesmerized me." *Taking away my choice!*

Mirceo's brows drew together. "Caspion, I did not. I don't possess that ability."

"You must have. I'm straight. Why would I want another male?"

"Because our minds are synced. Because we care for each other. Our friendship has grown into more."

"No, that doesn't explain . . ." *My explosive lust.* For Cas, a male who required control in all things, this situation was terrifying. He tried to say more but his throat felt too constricted.

Can't breathe. His gaze darted. *ESCAPE.*

"Calm yourself, demon, and think about this. You can't leave. My uncle Trehan will find you, and he will kill you. He carries death in his pocket."

Trehan Daciano. Cas had met the centuries-old Prince of Shadow this week. The grim, unsmiling assassin always carried his weapon—a sword with a crossguard in the shape of a crescent moon—and he was notoriously skilled with it.

But if Mirceo didn't reveal details, how could that soulless bastard find a single demon of no importance? Cas could return home and try to regain some semblance of his life.

ESCAPE NOW.

Mirceo raised his palms. "I can help you. Just give me time to figure this out. Let me help you."

"Don't tell Trehan where I live, Mirceo." Cas tensed to trace. "You owe me this after what you've done." *You made me a mindless slave. You took away my choice, my control.*

Sadness filled Mirceo's gray eyes. "They know when someone leaves. Trehan will find and kill you before dawn—"

Cas teleported away. An instant later, he materialized into his small loft in Abaddon. *What have I done?* Sweat covering him, he leaned against his door, about to vomit. Paranoia gripped him by the throat. *Kill me before dawn?*

No, no. Mirceo would never tell his uncle where to find Cas. Hell, Mirceo never listened to him, probably didn't even know Cas hailed from a backwater dimension like Abaddon.

Claws digging into the door, he struggled to process this night. He'd come with Mirceo, harder than he knew was possible. *And I'd still craved more of him—*

Commotion sounded from a nearby thoroughfare. He crossed to a window and cautiously peeked out. The swampy hamlet he'd left a month ago was packed with various Loreans.

They milled about like tourists. Why would anyone visit *this* place?

He traced out to the street and addressed a ferine demon gnawing on a pheasant leg. "What's the occasion that brings so many here?"

"Death-match tournaments in the old Iron Ring," the male said with excitement. The notorious cage arena of Abaddon hadn't been used in ages. The demon took another bite, saying, "Competitors—demons, trolls, Lykae, you name it—are teleporting in from all over the Lore. Understandable, considering the prize."

"Which is?" Cas asked, but he had a sinking suspicion in his gut. There were only two things in Abaddon that others might fight for.

"Whoever wins gets the *crown* of this entire demonarchy! Oh, and the hand of the princess." The male spat out a bone and walked on.

Bettina, no. A godsdamned troll could win her hand! Her guardians must have browbeaten her until she'd agreed to this.

I could enter the tournament. Could save her. A sense of being watched lifted the tiny hairs on the back of his neck. Was a killer already loose in Abaddon? *I could enter, if I live till morning. . . .*

SIX

Last outpost before the Plane of Lost Years
SEVERAL MONTHS—OR CENTURIES?—LATER . . .

Mirceo was on the hunt.

As he moved through the smoky, rough-neck tavern, he grinned to himself. *I, Mirceo Daciano, am* chasing *my fated one.*

But he had good reason. Unlike most vampires, he knew his mate's identity in advance of his blooding, and he was overjoyed with fate's choice for him.

Weeks ago, when his heart had gone still in his chest for good, Mirceo had visited Balery, the new king's fey oracle, and asked her when he would meet his mate. After rolling her bones, she'd blinked up at him and said four words that would change Mirceo's life forever: *You've already met him.*

Him. There'd been no question to whom Balery had referred.

Most often a male's mate would be a female. *But not always.*

His pairing with Caspion struck him as bloody brilliant. Nothing had ever made so much sense to Mirceo—which meant his reservations about monogamy and matehood had subsided.

His grin deepened. *I'm now a believer in the system.*

Caspion had once asked him, "What male wouldn't rush head-long to meet his beautiful mate?" *Indeed, demon. Indeed.* Mirceo was ready to commit.

Now he just needed to find Caspion. Blocking out the excruci-ating sound of a tinny violin, Mirceo scanned the crowded tavern. *Where are you . . . ?*

He'd heard Caspion planned to head to the Plane of Lost Years—a savage, war-torn dimension where time moved differ-ently—for some kind of self-exile.

Over my walking-dead body.

Their separation had gone on long enough. He wanted his best friend back—while expanding a few . . . *parameters* of their relationship.

Ignoring all the looks of interest he received from myriad immortals—*I'm quite taken*—he squared his shoulders, scarcely believing he'd soon be blooded. Once he spotted his mate, his heart would thud back to life. His lungs would fill with breath, and he would get hard as rock. . . .

But as he surveyed the crowd, a rare whisper of doubt arose. What if Caspion *wasn't* the male Balery had referred to?

No, no. Mirceo wanted Caspion to be his mate. Ergo, fate would comply. Such was how things worked for him.

Yet what if the demon stubbornly resisted the bond between them? And Trehan might have damaged Mirceo's chances with Caspion beyond repair. Both the demon and Trehan had entered the infamous Iron Ring of Abaddon—only one had been able to walk out.

Mirceo didn't see the demon among all the beings here. Strange. The locating crystal he'd used had indicated Caspion was inside this structure. Though Mirceo's senses weren't as keen as a demon's, he inhaled. . . .

He picked up the subtle thread of Caspion's unforgettable scent—

There! The demon was sitting alone at a table in the shadows, lost in thought.

Mirceo's brows drew together. Caspion seemed much changed. His careless, tousled hair was longer, and his normally clean-shaven face now had a golden shadow beard. His midnight-blue eyes seemed more . . . knowing. His body appeared to have grown, his shell-colored horns as well.

His appearance was edgier.

Darker.

That tournament in Abaddon had done something to Caspion, changing him.

Mirceo stared down at his chest. He wanted to change too, but his heart was still. His lungs took no breath. His cock was as hard as pudding.

No. It must be Caspion. He knocked a fist against his chest. *Come on, heart . . . awaken!*

Nothing.

Despite the patrons all around, Mirceo rubbed his member. *Get stiff, you traitorous thing.*

Not a twitch.

A buxom brunette demoness joined Caspion then, perching on his knee. Mirceo scowled. The female was all over him, peering up at the blond Adonis with an expression Mirceo had often received himself: *I wore my pretty panties tonight, so let's fuck.*

A last lay before the demon left for the Plane of Lost Years?

Mirceo choked back a surge of jealousy. He'd never known this strangling emotion before he'd met Caspion—

A massive, behorned tavern-goer lurched near Caspion's table, sloshing brew from a tankard the size of a vat.

Drawing the brunette out of the way, Caspion shot to his feet, saving her from a good dousing. "Watch what you're about," he grated to the giant.

Unbelievably, that male was at least a foot taller than Caspion. "Or what?" he snapped.

The horns of each demon breed differed. Was that giant a *stone demon*?

Caspion's own horns straightened with aggression. "You need to back away." Surely he wouldn't brawl with a stone demon. That breed could tense their muscles until their bodies became like stone. If Caspion threw a punch against that male, he'd break his hand. "You do not want to do this with me tonight."

"Do what? Kick your ass and steal your whore? Maybe that's just what I want to do."

Conversations dimmed, the violin going quiet. Sensing a fight, tavern-goers jockeyed for a better view.

When the giant's towering companions lined up behind him, Mirceo wended through the crowd to back his own friend.

In a menacing tone, Caspion told the giant, "I know your type. Though you've got no hope of getting laid, you need to assert your dominance. You need to yell, to heave your breaths, to feel *anything*. But this fight will not give you what you seek."

The stone demon's brows drew together. Seeming to see reason, he held up his free hand and backed away.

Sounds of disappointment rippled through the tavern.

Caspion turned to the female—

The giant tossed his tankard, soaking Caspion's chest in cheap brew, then he tensed for a fight.

Caspion still attacked, his fist flashing out with uncanny speed. It connected with the giant's jaw.

Mirceo's lips parted when that demon's face *fractured* like stone.

The giant collapsed to his back—unconscious and broken. His companions cast shocked looks at Caspion, then scattered like rats.

Glorious male! Caspion's damp shirt clung to his flexing muscles, his eyes gone black with ferocity.

Look at me, demon. Surely Mirceo's heart would start once he met gazes with such a warrior!

Though Caspion had won the fight, even more tension stole over him as he turned toward Mirceo. His tousled hair tumbled over one of his eyes, and he impatiently raked it back. Their eyes met. . . .

Nothing.

Mirceo's dormant heart sank.

SEVEN

Cas had scented Mirceo just as that stone demon hit the floor.

After so long, the mere sight of his former friend sent Cas reeling.

The vampire stood in the middle of the tavern, his bearing an equal mix of arrogance and elegance. He wore leather breeches and a trench coat—with no shirt. Only a prince like Mirceo could pull off that look. Among the rabble here, he looked like an angel, too perfect to be real.

A *fallen* angel; as he ogled Cas, Mirceo rubbed his tongue over one fang.

Cas had wondered if their . . . encounter would cool Mirceo's attraction or make it burn even hotter. The vampire's smoldering expression left no doubt in his mind.

Even after all this time, that look affected Cas. He could kill this smirking prince for what he'd done. For what he was *still* doing. Mirceo's needy moans and abandoned words from that last night in Dacia forever rang in Cas's ears: *I've dreamed about this, beautiful. Ride me! Use me, demon. Use me to come.*

Gritting his demon fangs, Cas strode through the tavern toward the exit, beings darting out of his way. He passed the vampire without another look, then shoved open the door, taking it off the hinges.

Outside, he crossed to a rickety fence that edged a viewing platform. In the valley below was the portal to the Plane of Lost Years, a.k.a. Poly. The large rift between dimensions shimmered with welcome, giving no hint of the hellhole that lay beyond—sweltering during the day, bone-chilling at night, and rife with violence.

As he watched, Loreans stepped through the portal to the other side. *Gods help you all.*

Sucking in the cold night air, Cas struggled to control his thundering heart. He caught the scent of sandalwood just before he heard a raspy voice: "You won't spare a word for your friend?"

Cas's shoulders tensed. Friend? *More like betrayer.* He'd believed Mirceo would intercede with his uncle. Instead, the spoiled prince must've told the assassin how to find Cas.

Trehan had descended upon Abaddon the same night Cas had fled Dacia.

Mirceo joined him at the fence, gazing out over the portal. "I can't believe you fractured a stone demon. I always loved to watch you fight—when I wasn't battling by your side—but what you just did was spectacular."

Before the fight, Cas had been lost in thought, wondering why he felt no satisfaction with his life. He'd had coin in his pocket, a drink in hand, and a buxom brunette ready to go back to his lodgings here at the outpost. *Life was good.*

So why wouldn't this emptiness in his chest ease?

The female had been just his type—a comely demoness with generous curves and a submissive disposition, who'd be all too happy to let him dominate her. Yet Cas had felt zero anticipation for what he'd thought to experience.

Life was good indeed—he'd worked his ass off to change his entire existence—so when would it *feel* good?

Maybe when he'd reclaimed the honor he'd lost in the Iron Ring? Cas turned to Mirceo. "How did you find me here?"

"I heard you were heading to the Plane of Lost Years—for some kind of self-inflicted punishment—and figured you'd stop at this outpost for a last lay."

You're a little late, prince. Cas had already been there for centuries, now returned. As a death demon, he derived strength from his every kill, and he'd made thousands on Poly; at last he was ready to fight Trehan again. Cas had simply needed a way to send a challenge to Dacia.

Which meant Mirceo's presence might actually be a boon.

"I was right as usual," the vampire continued. "I'm well aware of your immense sexual appetites, because I enjoyed them."

Cas shook his head. "You watched me with *females*."

"We watched each other. And then there was the night of our kiss."

That night had fucked Cas up for ages! He had never desired another male before or since Mirceo. "Just tell me why you're here."

"Testing a theory." The vampire's gaze rose. "Look at your gorgeous horns, Caspion."

The way Mirceo said his name was like a graze of lips across his throat, making Cas's pulse race. Godsdamnit, what hold did this male have over him? *I'll fight it to the death!*

Mirceo continued in that hypnotic voice, "I loved to watch them straighten and swell, transfixed by the sight. I still fantasize about kissing them. Licking them. Clutching them as I straddle you, riding that mouthwatering shaft of yours."

Fucking seductive vampire! Now Cas would be picturing those mental images for another eternity. "What do you want?" he demanded, his words embarrassingly thick.

"Are you heading to the Plane because you're still in denial about what happened between us? I know how much it affected you."

"What your assassin uncle did in the tournament affected me!" Though Cas had known Bettina wasn't his fated one, he'd entered for her hand to save her from some of the more monstrous entrants.

One problem: Trehan Daciano had sensed his mate in Bettina. The ruthless assassin had entered as well.

"Was the tournament really so bad? You fought hard, and you made it to the very end. People loved you."

Cas clenched his fists.

"I secretly watched you win an early match. All the demonesses threw their garters at you, screaming for your attention. At first, I thought I was jealous of your acclaim, wanting it for myself. Then I realized I was jealous whenever you smiled at those females. You were obviously enjoying their adoration."

"Oh, I did enjoy it. It felt ungodsly good to be respected and adored by my people." Crowds had cheered for him, chanting his name. The same demons who'd disdained Beggar had called Cas *the first son of Abaddon*! Until the final round had pitted him against Trehan. "Yet then your uncle wiped the floor of the ring with my face!"

Trehan had been poisoned by persons unknown, but he must have suspected Cas and Bettina. In his rage, the Prince of Shadow had annihilated Cas.

Snippets of that match flashed through his memory.

Trehan hurtling me against the side of the Iron Ring. A rusty spike breaking off inside my skull. Unimaginable pain. Vision fading to black. Where will the vampire strike next??? Can't see! Can't hear over the roar of the crowd! Blindly taking the attack, helpless to fight back. The snap of bones as the beating went on. And on. Choking on blood and humiliation. Bile. My own people cheering for Trehan.

When it'd ended at last, a deafening silence had reigned. Then the Dacian had renounced Bettina in front of all, leaving Cas the "victor."

The Abaddonae believed—rightly—that in a match to the death, someone must die. Instead, Trehan had left him to live in shame. . . .

Mirceo didn't look disturbed by Cas's anger whatsoever. "How could you defend yourself against my uncle? He's a blooded Dacian—who happens to be a millennium older than you are." *Not anymore.* "Would it help if I told you Trehan regrets his actions?"

"He saw reason?"

"You haven't heard? He discovered a malicious squire had poisoned his blood mead. Trehan and Bettina are reconciled and happily wed now."

King Trehan of Abaddon? *Godsdamn it!* Though Cas had finally gotten strong enough to defeat his enemy, could Bettina bear it?

As if reading his mind, Mirceo said, "My uncle worries for his delicate Bride. She would be torn apart if you two fought." And she'd already been through so much.

So you'll just abandon your revenge after all these centuries? The agony of that spike embedding in his skull was nothing compared to the blistering disgrace that followed—in and out of the Ring.

Once Cas had healed, he'd been forced to attend the

tournament award ceremony. As he'd gazed out at the silent, grim-faced Abaddonae, one thought had echoed through his mind: *I've known hatred and disdain all my life—but never like this.*

He had accepted the crown, giving it right back to Bettina for her to rule alone. What else could he do after that but leave?

Cas's situation there wouldn't be changed in such a short time, but *he* was changed. He was stronger, wealthier, and wiser, had even taught himself to read. Cas had more control over his life than ever before.

He would contemplate his next steps with calm rationality. He now knew how to find Trehan; there was time. Either way, Cas had nothing more to say to Mirceo. "I want you out of my life."

Mirceo stepped closer. "That's not possible." He inhaled, seeming greedy for Cas's scent—

The vampire's eyes shot wide, as if he'd been thunderstruck. Then they opened even wider. He tilted back his head and mouthed to the sky, "Oh gods, thank you!"

Cas scowled, unable to hold back his question: "For what do you thank the gods?"

Mirceo faced him with a delighted look. "My fondest wish just came true." In a low tone full of hunger, he added, "Ah, sweetheart, what fun you and I shall have together."

Cas recalled those words from so long ago. As before, a shiver crossed his nape.

Baffled by Mirceo's behavior, he traced back to his lodgings in the dusty outpost hotel.

Alone, he fought to calm his racing pulse. *You're wiser. Stronger. Focused. You're in control.*

Heading to the bathroom, he peeled off his sodden shirt, leaving his skin sticky with brew. He turned on the shower as cold as the water could get, then stepped under the cascade.

Cas was no longer an easily beguiled pup—so why did that pull toward Mirceo remain? It'd even intensified! Other vampires had attempted to enthrall him over the years and failed.

But then, none of them had been a Dacian.

Infinite times, Cas had lain in his bed in Poly, replaying that last night in Dacia. He'd relived the madness that had overtaken him, the primal lust that had forced him to pin down his friend and grind his cock against the vampire's till they'd both come. *Use me, demon—*

"I could wash your back for you." *Mirceo?*

Baring his fangs, Cas snapped, "How did you find me in here?"

"Not important," Mirceo said, keeping his gaze raised. "I have a pressing matter to discuss with you. If you don't like what I have to say, then you can still head off on your ridiculous penance trip, whiling away your years in hell."

Cas gave a bitter laugh. "That so?" Ready to leave this outpost for good, he continued to wash. "There's nothing for us to discuss. Nothing."

"Aren't you even curious what I might say?"

"No," he lied. In the small bathroom, Mirceo's scent inundated him, lighting up his mind. His shaft was getting harder than it'd been since the last time Mirceo had fucked with Cas's head.

"You don't seem to be in any particular hurry to leave this realm." Lowering his voice, Mirceo said, "It's been weeks since you abandoned me. That's long enough." He eased closer to the shower. "Deep down you know it is. You're vacillating about your journey, aren't you, sweetheart? Is something anchoring you here, hmm? Perhaps you are hesitant to venture so far from *me?*"

Cas leaned out of the shower stall to meet Mirceo's eyes. "You arrogant asshole. I'm just *returning* to this realm. I've been gone for more than five hundred years. Five centuries without a thought of you."

EIGHT

*B*OOM . . . . . . *BOOM* . . . . *BOOM* . . . . *BOOM* . . .
Mirceo's heart pounded again. Then again. And again.
The demon has blooded me.

As horrifying as his walking-dead existence had been, this reawakening was miraculous! His lungs expanded for breath, his shaft filling with blood. He knew from others that he would soon grow mindless to lose his seed with his mate.

Mirceo could scarcely think over these new changes, but had Caspion just said he'd already gone, then returned? "Allow me a moment to get this straight." He struggled to keep his eyes up, to *not* follow the water sluicing down the rugged planes of Caspion's body. If Mirceo glanced down, he might lose all control and fall upon this demon. "Though only weeks have passed here, you've been away for half a millennium?"

Caspion's answer was a sneer.

"I see." They'd been around the same age before. Though the immortal demon would look no older, Caspion now had fifty decades on Mirceo. How extraordinary. "Any reason you chose now to return? Because you hit your limit of missing me?"

"I've returned because I've collected bounties and made kills for centuries. Now I'm strong enough and rich enough to do and have anything I want."

Sexy demon! This new, hard-edged darkness only fueled Mirceo's desire.

When Caspion turned off the shower, Mirceo traced to collect a towel, offering it. *Eyes up!* "Could I have been so mistaken about your attraction to me?" he asked, knowing he hadn't been. Right now chemistry sparked between them.

So how had Mirceo's mate lived without him for so long?

The demon snatched the towel out of his hands. "You were utterly mistaken about me."

Mirceo could tell he was lying. A first. Unfortunately, Caspion hailed from an archaic realm of demons who held outdated views about same-sex relationships. Mirceo had predicted some resistance.

After all, Caspion had grown up an orphan, longing all of his life for just two things: respect and a family. A male mate would bring Caspion no offspring—and in the demonarchy of the backward Deathly Ones—nothing but shame.

Though Caspion had never judged Mirceo for bedding males, those kinds of views had to be what was holding the demon back from their obvious yearning for each other.

What other obstacle could there possibly be?

Caspion began drying off, corded muscles flexing beneath his tanned skin. *Eyes up! Up!* Not looking was an impossible feat when Caspion's prodigious member was semihard, swaying with his movements. Veined, with a rose-colored crown, it jutted proudly from the golden hair at the base of the demon's root. *My fair, golden Adonis.*

Mirceo's fangs throbbed for that flesh, and his new breaths went shallow. He again asked himself a question he'd long pondered: *How to seduce the demon?*

Caspion knotted the towel around his waist. "Begone from my sight, leechling."

Leechling? *My mate is an older male now.* "If you truly want me gone, then make it worth my while. Spend one night with me." He'd always topped with other males, but considering how dominant Caspion was, Mirceo figured he'd be falling on that sword, as it were. "If you still want nothing to do with me, I vow to the Lore I'll never bother you again," he said, taking a huge risk. A vow to the Lore was an unbreakable one.

"I will never fuck you, vampire. I'm not built that way."

With each new beat of his heart, Mirceo grew harder and more impatient with Caspion's stubborn beliefs. If Mirceo's mate was the demon, the reverse was likely true as well.

Mirceo believed Caspion would lose his demon seal deep within a vampire's body. *Mine.* "Still believe your fated one will be female? Yet you didn't find her in our . . . five hundred years apart?"

"I know demons who waited millennia. It will happen for me."

Oh, it has. "I'm in a bit of a hurry, sweetheart." Mirceo's breaths had grown ragged. His chest felt like it'd explode, his control in shreds. "I won't be able to fight fair." He would use any means necessary, any weapon at his disposal. He licked a fang as a memory from their month together arose.

In one orgy, Caspion and Mirceo had watched in drunken amazement as a Horde vampire delivered frenzied orgasms to one partner after another—with naught but his bloodied fangs.

Mirceo murmured to Caspion, "Gods I wish biting was no longer taboo. I ache to experience it. I'd risk the memories for just one taste of flesh."

Caspion couldn't seem to look away from the scene, had grown stiff as steel. "No one can resist him."

Mirceo whispered in his ear, "I should drink you thus. I bet I could make you come before I took my fill."

Having to clear his throat, Caspion joked, "If you handled my horns at the same time, I might not even stop you."

Now Mirceo thought: *Sounds like a plan.* His first bite.

Caspion narrowed his eyes. "Fighting fair? What are you talking about?"

To take the demon's warm wine at last . . . Mirceo teleported behind him, seizing his horns with both hands to yank Caspion's head back. Bronzed skin gloved Mirceo's throbbing fangs as he pierced the demon's neck. *"Uhn!"*

"The fuck, vampire???"

Mirceo sucked. Found a hot, wet heaven.

"Ahhh!" A bellow burst from Caspion's lungs, vibrating Mirceo's sensitive fangs.

The demon's rich blood was as exquisite as everything else about him. It seared Mirceo's veins, expanding them—as if he'd never lived until the demon's essence flooded him.

I'll drink him forever.

"Ah, gods! Kill you for this!" Caspion reached back to grip Mirceo's hair. But instead of flinging him away, the demon shoved Mirceo's fangs even deeper. "Enjoy it, leech." Caspion's hips rocked. "Last time . . . you feed . . . from my body."

Mirceo released one horn to rip that towel away. Hand snaking around Caspion's hip, he grasped his mate's shaft. *Hard as granite.* He snarled against the demon's neck.

With a defeated groan, Caspion bucked into his grip. "Make me come, you prick. Make me come, make me come." With each thrust, Caspion's sculpted ass clenched.

Mirceo ground his engorged cock against it. Though desperate to penetrate Caspion, he would never push his luck thus. He planned to spill right in his pants with a smile on his face.

The demon's leather scent made him light-headed; his sultry blood made him drunk. Mirceo sucked, he ground, he jacked his mate. Pressure built and built. He imagined Caspion pounding into him with his thick, veined length—

Done.

Finished.

Mirceo couldn't hold back his seed, lost all sexual control. As his member began pumping cum inside his pants, he released his bite to throw back his head. He bellowed to the ceiling as he ejaculated, torrents so powerful he shuddered in awe.

The demon tensed against him, yelling, "Ah, gods, *gods*. About to come! *GODS!*" His rod grew scalding against Mirceo's palm as friction built. Caspion's chest heaved with breaths, his exhalations hoarse.

Mirceo rasped at his ear, "Fuck my fist, beautiful. Come hard for me."

Caspion's cock pulsed in Mirceo's grip as he culminated in his dry demon release. "FUCK! *COMING!*" Orgasming over and over, Caspion gave brutal demonic roars, shaking the small room till dust rained from the ceiling. . . .

Mirceo wanted this moment to last forever. As they drifted down from that high, he milked the last of his mate's release, then lazily fondled the demon's semihard shaft.

If Caspion had felt even a fraction of Mirceo's pleasure, the demon should be in love with him directly.

~

Cas twisted and flung himself out of the vampire's grip. "Now you *die*." He'd despised this smirking leech *before* he'd come his brains out.

Even as Cas shoved Mirceo against the tiled wall, part of him acknowledged a shameful truth.

He'd waited half a millennium to release like that.

Hate him! Cas drew back his fist and launched it at Mirceo's too-perfect face, telling himself he liked the grunt of pain that followed. So why had he pulled his punch?

Blood flowed from the vampire's lip. *My fucking blood!* Stolen from his pierced neck.

Mirceo made a show of licking his lips. "Ambrosia. I'll suck you till eternity, sweetheart."

"Never call me that again!" Another punch connected with Mirceo's jaw.

The vampire took it, seeming proud to accept the blow. "My mate's gotten wickedly strong. We'll make a great couple."

What was he talking about? Cas launched his fist with all his strength—

Mirceo traced to the side.

Cas plowed a hole into the wall. "Godsdamn it!" He snatched his fist back, then seized the vampire to belt punches against his stomach.

Mirceo finally struck, taking Cas unawares, right in the side of a horn. The vampire's hand fractured. "Ah, fuck me!"

Cas's head rang like a banged drum. With a bellow of fury, he lunged for Mirceo, tackling him through the doorway into the bedroom. As they crashed to the floor, Cas pummeled Mirceo's side.

Between grunts, Mirceo said, "You're ready . . . for round two . . . sweetheart?"

Cas frowned down. His cock was hardening for more, straining against Mirceo's stiff member. *What is happening to me?* Madness was overtaking him! Just like that night in Dacia.

"Not surprising . . . since we're . . . *mates.*"

Cas's blood ran cold. What he was hearing *couldn't* be right: Mirceo's thundering heartbeat. And the vampire was heaving breaths. "You were blooded while I was gone."

They'd both known Mirceo's heart would stop soon, his sexual ability ending with it. Now the vampire's body had awakened.

Mirceo shook his head. "Blooded tonight. By *you.*"

Cas released him with splayed fingers, then traced backward to stand. "What kind of trick is this?"

"No trick." Mirceo licked his bloody lips again and murmured, "Mmmm."

That savoring sound made Cas's rod jerk, and Mirceo saw it.

The vampire smirked through the blood. "I'm not the only one affected by our pairing." He made it to his feet, adjusting his clothes.

"I'm not *paired* with you!"

"No?" Mirceo gazed at Cas's erection, which appeared to be straining toward him. "Look at all that pearly pre-cum you're making for me."

Cas gaped at his now-foreign member. Pre-cum did in fact bead the crown—a sight he'd never seen. *Closest I've ever been to spilling semen.*

"I can scent what your seed will taste like, beautiful. You'll have to pry me away."

Cas couldn't catch his breath. *This isn't happening.* "We're both male."

"It sometimes occurs this way. I, for one, couldn't be happier with the mate fate chose for me. And you're clearly attracted to me."

How many times had Cas wondered: *Why only Mirceo? Why no other males?* "Because you've . . . you've mesmerized me!"

"One more time: I don't have that ability. Fault me for being supernaturally sexy—guilty as charged—but I'm no mind-controller."

Had the vampiric allure Cas resisted actually been his attraction to a mate? *No.* He refused this. "How would I not know you were mine all that time?"

"When beings are of different species, sometimes the mating instinct won't be triggered until they're both mature." Fuck, that was true. "I wasn't until my heart stopped and I became immortal. But you'd already gone by that time."

Most vampires went eons between the freezing of their hearts and their blooding. Naturally the spoiled prince had been spared that long drought! Everything had always fallen into his lap.

Not me. To give up all his dreams? To become one among Mirceo's conquests? He'd seen the broken hearts Mirceo left in his wake. Would Cas be like them, begging for another night with the prince?

Then you'll always be a beggar, Cas.

Never. "I might be your mate, but you will *never* be mine."

Squaring his shoulders, Mirceo said, "I won't rest until we're bonded. You're going to take my virginity and give me your demon seal in return." Even with his face beaten, he'd regained his princely arrogance. "I'll give you time to wrap your head around your new existence. But know this, sweetheart: I will make you ejaculate so hard your balls will plead for mercy."

He disappeared, saving Cas the humiliation of his involuntary growl.

NINE

Castle Dacia
The Realm of Blood and Mist

The next gloaming, Mirceo sauntered along the gallery overlooking the training yard and settled into an alcove to watch his sister at her sword practice.

Pride suffused him. She'd inherited her blistering speed—and her pointed ears—from some distant fey ancestress, but she'd earned her skill through constant training. Before long, Mina would be able to challenge even the great Trehan.

The protective diamond at the apex of this vast cavern cast filtered sun and prisms over the rambling kingdom. Rays beamed down over Mina, illuminating her white-blond hair. As she defeated one sparring partner after another—all of them much larger males—her blue eyes blazed with focus.

Whereas Caspion had midnight-blue eyes, Mina's were lighter, a crystalline ice blue.

Mirceo still couldn't believe he'd once thought those two might be a pair. As he watched her graceful moves, he cast his mind back to their meeting.

"Sister, may I present Caspion? He is my best and most treasured friend."

Faced with the demon's uncommon good looks, she blushed and stammered, unable to meet Caspion's gaze for more than a peek.

"Caspion, this is the princess Kosmina."

When she offered her hand, the demon took it and pressed a kiss to the back. "A pleasure, princess."

Had her cheeks ever been so red? "Yes. A p-pleasure." She was as bashful as Mirceo was shameless.

Though Mina was tongue-tied and adorable, the demon's eyes weren't lighting up. Caspion's expression could best be described as . . . fond.

As Mina's practice came to a close, the last clang of steel echoed over the courtyard. She must've sensed Mirceo's gaze on her. She peered up at him, her face glowing. Tossing her sword to a servant, she traced to Mirceo. "Your heart is beating!"

He swung her around in his arms. "It is, my darling Mina! I've been blooded, enjoying all that this milestone entails." His speed now rivaled hers, his senses more acute than ever. Little other than a beheading or unfiltered sunlight could kill him, and he regenerated even faster. His injuries from the night before had healed in mere hours. *No doubt helped along by Caspion's crimson ambrosia.*

Transforming himself into mist—a talent only Dacians possessed—would be much easier, and he'd be able to transform his mate as well.

"Already!" She suffered no reticence or awkwardness with her big brother. "How fortunate. Are you much stronger?"

"By a hundredfold."

"So it *was* Caspion! I knew it." Mina's innocent eyes gazed past Mirceo. "Where is he?"

Not with me. Yet. "Take a walk?"

She eagerly nodded, and they exited the castle perimeter to stroll down one of the cobblestone streets.

After a few moments, Mirceo admitted, "Caspion is being a touch resistant to the idea of me as a mate. Might've spurned me a bit."

Her blond brows drew together. "But he wasn't resistant to the idea of *me* as his mate."

In a dry tone, Mirceo said, "Believe me, I have moments when I wish I were your big sister."

"I meant, that he didn't mind my species. Or my diet."

"No, vampirism is not the obstacle." He should be so lucky. In order to have Caspion, Mirceo would've eaten food and lived like a demon—even though he'd regain pesky bodily functions and miss the hell out of blood and biting. *Gods, I would miss biting.* "My masculinity, however . . ."

"Please don't take this the wrong way, brother, but I don't think sweet Caspion would *spurn* you if you were everything perfect except for your . . . maleness."

Mirceo frowned. "Then by that reasoning, are you saying I'm *imperfect?*"

"I'm just saying other factors might be at work."

He exhaled a gust of breath. "Maybe I *am* seizing on the one thing I can't change—because I don't have the fortitude to change the things I can."

"That would mean evolving as a person." For such an innocent female, Mina could be surprisingly incisive. "Which would take work."

Perhaps Mirceo could be a touch less arrogant. Maybe a bit less vain. He could take things more seriously.

How boring I'd be! "Damn him, I like myself. All I want to do is be there for him. To get back to our enhanced friendship."

"Much has happened since then." In a lower voice, she added, "With his defeat in the Iron Ring. He must hate Trehan so much."

"After his trials, my mate might have . . . exiled himself. To the Plane of Lost Years."

Mina gasped. "How long was he there?"

"He spent five centuries away from me." Mirceo couldn't hide his hurt. The demon had invaded all of his thoughts and dreams, but Caspion hadn't even looked back.

Mirceo had half a mind to go see that place. If Caspion had stayed there so long, how bad could it truly have been?

"Five *hundred* years? Is he much changed?"

"I only spent a few moments with him—the blooding made me *insane*—but I suspect Caspion's boyish charm has disappeared forever. He's edgier and somehow . . . darker." Yet no less attractive. Just the opposite.

"Oh, Mirceo, what will you do?"

"I'll go to him tonight. Try to wear him down." *I, Mirceo Daciano, will run panting after another.* How the worm had turned!

"Will you be true to him?"

"Utterly."

She raised her brows.

"You doubt my faithfulness, sister? Just because I've never been monogamous before?" Mirceo let others believe that only his selfish need for conquests drove his appetites. Did he enjoy a good conquest? Of course; who didn't? But his situation was more complicated than that.

He'd never woken beside a partner without an inexplicable anxiety overtaking him, the need to escape another's clutches riding him.

Surely he wouldn't feel panic after Caspion claimed him. Their connection would cure Mirceo of that. Fate wanted them together.

"Be good to my new brother." Mina's eyes were filled with sympathy. "He's been through so much."

"That's why he needs *me*." As the last members of the House of Castellan—the heart of the Dacian kingdom—Mirceo and Mina were tasked with safeguarding the castle and all those within it. Maybe the need to care for others had been ingrained in them.

Mirceo wanted to safeguard his new mate, to soothe the worry from his brow.

As Mirceo and Mina passed one of Dacia's blood fountains, the scent reminded him.... "I drank from Caspion." Most Dacians eschewed bloodtaking because they didn't want anyone else's recollections to interfere with their clear, cold minds. As predicted, Lothaire—their newly installed regent—had denounced the bloodtaking taboo. In fact, the mad king *expected* his subjects to drink from others. "I took straight from my mate's neck."

Mina looked scandalized. Alas, Lothaire had been king for just a few months, and revolutions took time. "Will you see Caspion's memories?"

They would come in dreams, seeping into his consciousness. "I hope so." Mirceo's mind had never been clear and cold anyway. "I want to learn anything I can about my mate."

"What's your strategy to win him over?" An expert on martial tactics, Mina often viewed life through that lens.

"Play on his jealousy? Remind him how much fun we had together?" Caspion—a hunter—loved to collect bounties; perhaps he and Mirceo could bond over that interest.

"Do you have Uncle Trey's scry crystal?"

Mirceo reached into his coat pocket, knuckles brushing the talisman. "I used it last night." Trehan had regretted his rage against Caspion so much that he'd offered Mirceo the use of the priceless crystal.

Though Mirceo could locate Caspion anywhere in the worlds, he already had a good idea where the demon, a creature of habit, would be tonight.

Mina said, "I still can't believe you confided your mate's identity to Uncle Trey."

For centuries, backbiting conflict had plagued the Dacian royals. Mirceo and Mina's parents had been casualties. Now peace reigned—yet another change brought about by Lothaire. "It's nice not to continually expect a sword in the back," Mirceo said, an understatement. His personality had been shaped by paranoia.

Once that had faded, hedonism had been a welcome alternative.

He and Mina each fell into their own thoughts, strolling along in easy companionship. He raised his face to the diamond-filtered sunlight. *Vampire paradise.* All it lacked was Caspion.

Out of the corner of his eye, Mirceo saw Mina worry her bottom lip with a fang. His gaze locked on her face. "What's on your mind, sister?"

Her cheeks flushed. "You can always tell when aught is amiss with me."

Because he'd raised her from the time he was fifteen. "Go on."

"Do you know that I've never spoken to a strange male before?" As if this were a bad thing for a princess? "Everyone who comes into contact with me is vetted, then introduced. As Caspion was."

Mirceo *slept* with strangers every night. Or, rather, he had in the past. "So?"

"Uncle Lothaire spoke again about sending me outside of the kingdom."

The king considered her *too* innocent. Granted, Mirceo had sheltered her, possibly too much. But to dispatch Mina—who'd never seen a car or a skyscraper—outside the realm was ludicrous.

"I'm half terrified, half thrilled about the prospect," Mina said, her blue eyes alight.

Mirceo shook his head. "It's too dangerous. Do you forget that a deadly plague still spreads in the otherlands? There's a reason no vampiresses exist out there." The plague struck females especially hard.

"But if I remain in my mist, I can't be touched by it," Mina pointed out. "I would go out and secretly investigate, as you and the others always do. *Forever to observe, never to engage.*"

Mirceo had broken that rule more times than he'd followed it. "Absolutely not."

"But Uncle Lothaire says it's time for us to open our borders and interact with other Loreans."

Among other radical changes, the mad king had relaxed all travel restrictions. He even planned to lift the veil of Dacian secrecy, bringing the kingdom out of hiding.

"This is my final word on the subject, sister. I will speak with Lothaire." Mirceo didn't relish the idea. Though the Dacianos had brought the rightful heir into the realm to rule, the three-millennia-old Enemy of Old had proven to be a handful. "Somehow I will make him see reason. Or I'll prevail upon our queen if necessary." Lothaire's vampire mate, Elizabeth, was a former human, a tough-as-nails mountain girl he'd turned immortal.

It hadn't been so long ago when she'd nearly decapitated Lothaire during one of their fights—which, knowing Lothaire, had been a justified response. Once he'd healed, the king had cut out his own heart and mailed it to her as a kiss-off. She'd severed her middle finger and mailed it back in salutations.

With his red eyes merry, the Enemy of Old had once summed up their courtship: "There was *drama*."

If those two could get past their matehood issues, surely Mirceo and Caspion could. He told Mina, "Elizabeth will back me on this."

Lothaire worshipped his "hellbilly" queen, and her influence over him was substantial. Mirceo had seen them together just this morning in one of the castle's shadowy nooks. Lothaire had stroked Elizabeth's mink-brown hair behind her ear as he'd gazed into her eyes. "You are everything," he'd said simply.

She'd sighed, "I'm sweet on you too, Leo."

Mina stopped in the street. "Brother, please just consider the possibility." Her eyes glinted. "I feel like . . . like I'm slowly dying down here."

"As opposed to quickly dying out there?" At the thought of losing her, his lungs seemed to contract. *I couldn't survive it.* He just prevented himself from digging his black claws into his chest.

He had adored his mother and father. Though they'd been formidable immortals in their prime, they'd perished easily enough.

Mirceo would lock Mina in the dungeon before he lost another loved one. He pinned her gaze. "Mark my words, Kosmina Daciano, you will not be leaving this kingdom for centuries to come. . . ."

TEN

New Rome Pleasure Palace

W hich female would you like, sir?" the palace purveyor, a vampire/fey halfling, asked Cas. "All of them are available, except for the two on the settee." He gestured toward a pair of busty, redheaded nymphs. Just Mirceo's type.

Stop thinking about him.

Cas had tried to keep busy today, checking on the apprenticeships he'd set up before he'd left for Poly. Now he was able to fund as many as he liked, benefitting even more pups in Abaddon.

For some reason, he'd never told Mirceo about working with those foundlings.

Stop. Thinking. About. Him. Easier said than done; Cas had first met the vampire in this very place, a usual haunt of Cas's when he'd been in his twenties—mere months ago on this plane.

He gazed over the line of remaining females. Demonesses, succubae, nymphs . . . He finally had the finances to pay for his shadow life, yet all he could think about was Mirceo's promise to make him ejaculate till his balls pled for mercy.

And just like that, Cas's shaft stirred. All day, he'd wondered how Mirceo would find him. A blooded vampire would not take separation from his . . . *fated one* lightly.

Cas still couldn't believe he'd blooded his former friend. Or that the vampire had bitten him! Now the arrogant prince could dream his memories. Every demeaning one.

Last night, Cas had peered in the mirror at the healing bite on his neck, tracing it with a sick captivation. In a way, Mirceo had marked him, which had alternately infuriated and aroused Cas.

He'd stroked off repeatedly, gritting his teeth against the pleasure that prick had forced on him. *Focus, Cas.*

Demonesses, succubae, nymphs . . . Yet none of those smiling beauties called to him—

A familiar scent hit Cas. Mirceo was here? *Chasing me again!*

"Fancy meeting you here," the vampire said as he strode into the salon. He wore even tighter leather breeches and a form-fitting white shirt that highlighted his teeth and fangs.

The ones that were shoved inside me last night. Cas grew rockhard. "Do you think to stop me from enjoying myself here?"

"*Stop* you?" Mirceo flashed him a confused glance. "I'm here for myself. I've got two females on reserve. I can indulge in my old pastimes now that you've blooded me and awakened my body once more. I mean, look at me, Caspion"—he gestured at himself—"*someone* should be enjoying all this perfection." *So sly, so bloody seductive.*

Cas's heart pounded in his ears.

The vampire's gaze dipped to Cas's groin, then back up. "Careful, sweetheart, your eyes are turning black with rage."

Cas heard the females whispering:

"Mirceo's already been blooded!"

"The demon and the vampire are mates!"

"Would've loved to see their claiming."

"To be the jam in that sandwich!"

There'd been no claiming! Turning to the purveyor, Cas said, "I'll take those." With a careless wave, he indicated a succubus with purple hair and a dark-eyed nymph, then chanced a glance at Mirceo.

He could swear the vampire's expression was . . . hurt, before Mirceo masked it with a smirk. Cas coldly turned from him, allowing the females to lead him down the hallway to a chamber. Inside the luxurious room was an oversize bed and a plush divan. "On the bed, ladies. You two get started for me."

He sat on the divan, needing to get lost in sex. But as he watched the smiling pair begin to kiss, his thoughts drifted, and instead he got lost in memories of that fateful night in Dacia. . . .

One more taste, then he'd end this. One more dip into this unfamiliar well. . . .

Yet soon raw lust overwhelmed curiosity. He slanted his mouth over the vampire's, demanding more. Their tongues twined, their breaths gone ragged. My gods, this feels so fucking good.

Dimly, Cas realized the giggling females were closing the bedroom door behind them.

He roused, his mind struggling to come back online. Mirceo's moan slammed him right back into this kiss.

Just one last taste . . .

Some foreign mix of emotions welled up inside Cas. Lust. Yearning. Tenderness warred with aggression.

So much godsdamned aggression. Need to control this! To control Mirceo. *He overpowered his friend, pinning the vampire's wrists above his head.*

When Mirceo sucked on his tongue, Cas's mind was sucked

free of thought—until all he could do was feel every searing sensation.

His horns ached in a way they never had before. Even his fangs ached. His dark claws sharpened, and he had the impulse to sink them into Mirceo's flesh, holding the vampire steady for his use.

Cas's control faltered, no match for this pleasure. He loosened his grip on Mirceo's wrists, but only to seize the vampire's lean hips. Growling into their kiss, Cas thrust, grinding his rod against Mirceo's.

The prince thrust his hips upward, meeting Cas. Seeming mindless, he dug his claws into Cas's back, spurring that demonic aggression.

Kissing . . . kissing, they bucked and writhed, shoving hips, rocking cocks. Pressure built. Cas's shaft throbbed from it. Pain. Bliss. Pain. *Every one of Mirceo's helpless moans ratcheted up the brutal intensity.*

Against his lips, Mirceo rasped, "About to spill in my pants! Don't stop!" Cas drew his head back to witness the vampire in the throes. Mirceo's smoldering gray eyes had turned black with need. *"I've dreamed about this, beautiful. Ride me! Use me, demon. Use me to come. Do it.* Ah, gods, DO IT—"

Mirceo's back bowed. "AHHHH!" Head thrashing, he began to ejaculate; Cas could scent it.

The vampire's hot, creamy seed.

That scent hurled Cas over the edge. He was going to culminate with this male harder than he ever had before. Heart thundering, he tensed as if to take a blow.

His release was a detonation.

He threw back his head and roared to the ceiling. Bliss radiated throughout every inch of his body from his scalp to his curling toes. His mind turned over. His heart in his chest.

Pleasure had bested him. The hunter had been slain. . . .

Cas shook his head hard. *Beat this obsession.* Sex beckoned mere feet away. His females for the night had started leisurely sixty-nining.

A pair of courtesans going down on each other would normally put him in a lather to join in. But the sight did little to soothe his agitation.

Two options: I'm bisexual, or Mirceo is somehow enthralling me. In Poly, Cas had encountered males that others considered attractive and felt nothing. Yet just recalling the scent of Mirceo's cum made his cock throb.

His head snapped around when the vampire's voice sounded from the hallway. A nearby door opened and closed. Mirceo's low, accented words came from the next room over.

He would be bedding two nymphs on the other side of that wall.

Will I hear him spending? Those females screaming?

Damn him! Cas refused to allow Mirceo to ruin this for him. He *would* join the two panting courtesans in bed, taking them so long and loud that the vampire never doubted Cas was free of him forever. . . .

ELEVEN

My plan isn't working out as intended.

Mirceo paced, crazed at the thought of his mate with another. With *others*. Yes, the demon had bedded countless females before, as had Mirceo . . .

But now he's blooded me. Now he's brought me back to life.

Mirceo's own dates lay unclothed on the large bed, marveling at his behavior. He might've thought he would miss lush breasts and curvy bodies—he'd desired females and males equally—but now all he wanted was one very stubborn demon.

Even an immortal like Mirceo had to strain to hear sounds in the next room. These walls were thick by design. *Want to see him!*

The Dacians were secret observers; tonight Mirceo would return to form. Planning to test his enhanced abilities, he whispered to the nymphs, "Back in a moment." He traced into the hall, then transformed into mist. Invisible, scentless, he flowed into Caspion's room, merging with the wall.

The demon sat on a divan, lost in thought. He didn't seem to register what the females were doing to each other—though their wantonness was brow-raising.

Ah, the play of emotions on Caspion's face: lust, misery, then wrath. The demon clenched his fists and stood, staring in the direction of Mirceo's room.

I need something to spur him into action. But what? *Ah, yes . . .* Withdrawing as invisibly as he'd entered, he returned to his own room. "Ladies," he told his nymphs, "I'll pay a fortune in gold if either of you can amuse me." He feigned a bored yawn. "Make me laugh." Whenever he and Caspion had gone out carousing, they'd often laughed for hours. Caspion had once drunkenly admitted, "I like your laugh, vampire. Rubs me on the inside." If the demon heard Mirceo's amusement now . . .

Rising to the challenge, one of the nymphs recited a bawdy limerick. Mirceo did laugh. Loudly.

Five . . . four . . . three . . . two—

Caspion appeared and lunged for Mirceo, tracing him in midair. Suddenly, they were outside the palace in the damp night. The rolling green hills all around were covered with dew. The waxing moon hung heavy above.

Caspion shoved him against the exterior wall, cracking the bricks. "I could kill you for this!"

Mirceo drawled, "Decided to get me alone all to yourself?" For the first time, he was attracted to a warrior who could overpower *him*, a Dacian, and make him submit. Surprisingly, that thought got Mirceo hard as stone.

Who knew?

Behind Caspion, a palace sentinel exited to check out the commotion, but Mirceo waved him away. Attention back on the demon, he said, "All you had to do was ask."

~

"You want to ruin everything I enjoy? *Why?*"

"When was the last time you enjoyed it?" the vampire demanded. "You took me from those females because you're jealous of me with others!"

I . . . am.

How? When had this bone-deep possessiveness taken hold? "You called me your mate, but the day after your blooding, you're right back in a brothel! Exactly as I'd expect."

"Because I knew you'd be here, you lout, and I wanted to provoke you." Moonlight shimmered over the vampire's face and eyes. The black ring around his light irises grew, onyx overwhelming gray.

Spellbinding me.

Had Cas earned all his new strength only to be helpless against this male? *Never.* Cas snapped his fangs. His horns straightened, half in lust, half in fury.

Mirceo's brows drew together. "Fuck, you get my cock hard when you go demonic."

Cas growled. He watched in disbelief as his hands shot out to seize the vampire's nape.

And then they were kissing, gnashing fangs, tongues tangling. *Madness.* How Cas had missed this madness! How much he hated it! His mind wasn't wandering; he was hyperaware of every detail, dialed in to the vampire's responses with a laserlike focus.

Never breaking their kiss, Mirceo reached down between them, fumbling with Cas's fly. In the cool night, he shoved Cas's pants to his knees. Then his own.

Cas jolted when heat seared him; their bared shafts had made contact. He hissed in a breath just as Mirceo lost his—they were even fucking breathing for each other!

Mirceo took both of their cocks into his hands, stroking them together. The sensations were unfamiliar. *But so good.*

He imagined what Mirceo's length would look like pressed against his own, and couldn't keep from bucking into the vampire's iron grip.

Was that Mirceo's pre-cum? *Or my own?*

Between kisses, the prince admitted, "You drive me insane with jealousy!"

Cas yanked Mirceo's hair free of its queue, then threaded his fingers through the length. "Get used to jealousy—because once this fever passes tonight, I *will* be with females."

Mirceo grazed a fang over Cas's jugular. "I'll never allow it."

Cas tilted his head back and stared up at the sky. "And you think to stop me?"

"Every time you're inside a female, I vow to the Lore I will be too."

Another growl erupted from Cas's chest. He peered down at Mirceo. "Then I'll chain you up somewhere, leech. A prisoner for my use. Keep you as my shameful little secret."

"If I say pretty please, sweetheart? Until that time, I won't just retaliate with females, I'll take males. Though I never have before, I will let *males* take *me.*"

A haze covered Cas's vision. Another male claiming the prince's virginity?

Mirceo read him so well, twisting the knife. "Whenever I fantasize about you and me, I'm usually the bottom, so I should get some experience."

Bottom. Fucking. Sinking deep into the vampire's sleekly muscled body.

Cas wrapped Mirceo's hair around his fist. Voice unrecognizable, he bit out, *"No. One. Takes. You."*

"No one but you?"

Cas could erase the vampire's smirk with just one thrust.

"You once told me you hate tempering your strength during sex. I'm a blooded Dacian; I can handle anything you can imagine. Any filthy fantasy can be yours."

I could bend him over, seize his pale hips, and shove into him right now. Mirceo would moan for it. *I could give him my cum.*

Cum? *Would* Mirceo break his seal?

Then Cas would have to accept this bond! "I will never fuck you," he swore, even as he sank his claws into Mirceo's bare ass. He'd never dared claw another.

The prince groaned. "Demon, *more.*"

Cas clutched him harder. They thrust and ground in a frenzy, and all the while Mirceo kept their shafts clenched together.

Heat spread. Friction burned, but Cas couldn't get enough. "So godsdamned good!" His horns and cock ached. His . . . fangs. A demon male would bite his mate during the claiming. His gaze flicked to Mirceo's neck.

The vampire noticed. "Want to leave your mark on me, beautiful? Claim me?"

"You can dream all you want; it will never happen."

"I do dream about it. Today I stroked off while I imagined suckling your exquisite cock. In my fantasy, I took you so deep that your golden curls tickled my nose." *Mercy!* "I didn't stop until you went mindless. Till you lost all restraint and fucked me like a demon in his prime."

Chasing his release, Cas thrust harder. "You've got me so twisted up inside!"

"Right before I came, I pierced my lip and sucked it for your blood. Because I'll never get enough of it." Mirceo's head shot forward.

Fangs sank into Cas's neck. *"Ahhh!"* Pleasure exploded. That bite ruled him, rocked him. His veins felt searing hot, his blood seething to be freed. "Enjoy it for the last time, leech—"

Mirceo sucked.

Cas's eyes rolled back in his head. *So . . . fucking . . . good.*

The vampire snarled into his bite, lean body going tense.

Cas's eyes widened when wet heat spurted over their cocks. "*Uhn!* Feel your hot cum!" Out of his mind, he fucked Mirceo's tight, slippery grip. "I *scent* it!" Cas started to orgasm, his shaft jerking against Mirceo's. "Coming . . . *COMING!*"

The vampire released his bite just as Cas threw back his head and bellowed to the night sky. *"Yes, yes, YES!"* Pulsations seized him. Again and again, he thrust to milk every last ounce of pleasure.

Bliss and wonder made Cas float.

Only the vampire kept him from drifting away.

TWELVE

After-shudders racked the demon's powerful body.

Mirceo clutched him and experienced each one with him. Their breaths heaved in sync, their hearts pounding in rhythm.

His lids slid shut as he savored this closeness. These days, he wouldn't be happy unless every part of him was in contact with every part of this stubborn demon. He wanted their limbs entangled, blood and cum shared.

With a last dazed groan, Caspion nuzzled Mirceo's ear and neck, continuing to slowly thrust.

Mirceo's member was hypersensitive, so he loosened his grip a degree, but the demon's growl had him tightening his fingers again. With a grin, he murmured, "Shall I lick clean the mess I made down there, sweetheart?"

Tension stole over Caspion, the spell broken. Soon the demon would shove away from him, blasting accusations, denying the obvious.

Maybe Mirceo should make sure Caspion's addiction matched his. When the demon pried himself away, Mirceo swiped his cock-head for his own seed. *Time to give the demon a taste of what he's missing.* . . .

Hauling his pants up over his still-hard shaft, Caspion stumbled back against the wall, knees seeming to buckle.

Mirceo understood. When he'd been bloodtaking, his fangs must've been the only things holding him upright. Now he barely got his own pants in place.

Caspion slid down to sit, so Mirceo teleported over, straddling the demon's lap. "Look at me, beautiful." Mirceo curled a finger under his chin.

Resentment gleamed in Caspion's stormy-blue eyes. "You won this round. What more do you want?"

"For you to think about one thing. If no other being in all the worlds is to lay claim to me but you, then what does that make me . . . ?"

~

Mine.

Sly vampire! Mirceo had opened the door to that kind of thinking, giving a voice to Cas's possessiveness.

Mine.

Mine.

Mine.

As if Cas had spoken aloud, Mirceo said, "Uh-huh. Yours. Fate connected us, demon. Surrender to the pull."

"Never."

"Then give me one final kiss." Mirceo leaned in and took Cas's lips in a lazy, wet kiss.

Too weak to resist him. Last night, unfamiliar pathways in Cas's brain and body had seemed to open for the first time. Tonight was no different. About to start the madness all over again, Cas tasted his own blood and something else, some delectable thread. . . .

He yanked his head away. "You prick!" He shoved Mirceo off him and traced to his feet. "You painted your lips with your cum, so I'd taste it?"

From his spot on the ground, Mirceo grinned, his eyes dancing. "Yes."

"You want to take me over, to seep into me."

Mirceo traced to stand. "As you've done to me."

If the vampire *was* in fact his mate and Cas refused to claim him, his demon instincts would become more explosive, growing apace with his surging aggression. Already he felt out of control. *Dangerous.*

How had things devolved so quickly? In this realm, it'd only been months since they'd been laughing and reveling together— since Mirceo had read to him in the still of the morning.

Cas had changed; Mirceo . . . hadn't.

The vampire had *forced* him into this situation. That prince had never experienced what it was like to have no choice, to be doomed to a single outcome.

To be helpless.

All of Cas's actions had been directed toward one goal: to wield control over his own destiny. He'd had no choices when orphaned. Just to eat, he'd been forced to do things no child should ever contemplate. He'd had no choices when others had scorned him for his poverty.

Now Mirceo was hemming him in once more. Either the vampire had no clue what his tricks were doing to him—or the selfish prince just didn't give a fuck.

Cas paced. "Tell me how to be rid of you."

"I did. Claim my body, and if you still don't want me, I vow to the Lore I'll never bother you again."

"That won't happen," Cas said, even as he wondered if he should simply take what Mirceo offered and lose his seal. Then he could find a female to have younglings with.

Could he fuck another male? The mere idea of sinking inside Mirceo made his body vibrate. If Cas went into one of those mindless rampages, he would be inside the prince within a heartbeat's time. He'd wrench moans out of that vampire, dominating him.

Putting the arrogant prince on his hands and knees. Such a vulnerable position. Cas rubbed the heel of his palm over his shaft.

His only physical issue with taking Mirceo? Cas feared he'd come prematurely. "I just want you *gone*."

"And what if you change your mind? How would you ever be able to find me?"

Though a demon could teleport to places he'd previously been, some kind of esoteric Dacian magic dimmed memories of the kingdom's location. Even a tracker like Cas could never reach Dacia again. Not that he'd ever wanted to remember how to return to that cursed place!

"Caspion, you would be mired in regret."

"I'll show as much regret as *you* did when your uncle set off to assassinate me. Thanks for the warning!"

Gray eyes narrowed. "I warned you *before* you left, sweetheart. And before you even journeyed to Dacia! But the threat of death didn't slow you down, did it? Because what happened between us was so powerful that you had to flee what you felt."

Cas couldn't argue with that. "Say that's true. You could've requested leniency for your friend."

"Ah, my *friend*? The one who betrayed the laws of my people?

In any case, I did ask for leniency. I pleaded for it. But I was granted none. So I acted resigned, even as I plotted to do whatever it took to protect you."

If true—and natural-born vampires couldn't lie—then this news appeased at least some of the rage he felt toward Mirceo. All these years, Cas had carried that burden.

As it dissipated, numbness took its place.

"When Trehan came for you that night, I was already in Abaddon, ready to defend you," Mirceo said. "You remained in a godsdamned brothel till morning."

Cas's lips parted. He *had* been there. Mirceo had planned to challenge the great Prince of Shadow? Which meant Mirceo had intended to risk his very life. *For me.*

"But my uncle never made it to you because he sensed Bettina and was distracted. Then he entered the tournament." For her, Trehan had left his mist in front of thousands, turning his back on his kingdom. "I couldn't interfere with anything after that point."

"Do not remind me." Those tournament rules had governed all of their behavior inside and out of the ring. "Did you see Trehan fight me?" *Say no . . .*

"No, I didn't. My other uncles and I were chasing our new king all over the Lore, trying to protect him and Queen Elizabeth, his mate." Rubbing his nape, Mirceo added, "But I heard about it."

Cas's face heated. "The Abaddonae will never view me the same way. Trehan denied me an honorable death." Since his self-exile, Cas still wasn't ready to face the people of his kingdom.

Though I miss Bettina. He hadn't seen her in centuries.

"Honorable death?" Mirceo scoffed. "You can't enjoy honor when you're dead."

Cas didn't bother arguing with him; a spoiled prince like

Mirceo would never understand. "Did you tell Trehan that I'm your mate?"

"I did."

Cas's worst enemy now knew his greatest weakness. "And how did you reveal that? Did you refer to me as your Bride? Is that how you would introduce me?"

"I see the blood rise in your cheeks." Mirceo exhaled with impatience. "Our species has always been inclusive, and now we are updating the terminology. Male or female, a mate is a mate," he said. "Besides, as a prince of Dacia—which you already are, just by virtue of our fated connection—you won't be introduced to others. They will be *presented* to you, because you are now a royal of the House of Castellan, the heart of our kingdom."

"Me? A prince?"

Mirceo nodded. "Mina and I are all that's left of our house. We need you, Caspion—"

"Shut up." Awareness lifted the fine hairs on Cas's nape. The rolling hills surrounding the brothel were *too* still. Insects and night creatures had fallen silent. He surveyed the terrain. One by one vampires materialized in the distance.

"No need to be rude, you lout." Mirceo sighed. "But if I must, I'll polish your manners along with your knob."

Cas rolled his eyes. "Vampires close in on us." They emanated menace. *Excellent.* He needed to vent some frustration.

Mirceo inhaled the air, catching the same smells. With a grin, he said, "Do you remember our nights of bloodshed, sweetheart?"

"Stop calling me that!"

Unperturbed, Mirceo said, "Our new opponents don't smell like Horde vampires. Could be Forbearers. They might be here for me, since King Lothaire abducted and imprisoned Kristoff, their king."

Wait, Lothaire? "The Enemy of Old is the king your family crowned?" By all accounts, Lothaire was as deranged as he was vicious.

"He's the rightful heir."

"Why in the gods' names would Lothaire kidnap Kristoff?"

Shrug. "Uncle needed someone to play chess with."

"Your entire bloody family is insane."

"Fair point. I believe the imprisonment also stems from the fact that Kristoff is Lothaire's secret half brother, on his father's side. The *Horde* side. For all we know, this might be Lothaire's way of bonding." Growing more serious, Mirceo said, "Those Forbearers will have swords, and we do not."

Cas bared his fangs and claws, sneering, "I'll have a sword soon enough."

"Yes, of course." Mirceo jutted his chin. "As will I."

Half a dozen vampires appeared not fifteen feet away, forming a rough semicircle, weapons raised. They had clear eyes. Forbearers. That order of turned humans took a vow never to drink blood from the flesh.

The largest male, the apparent leader of the troop, said, "As predicted, Mirceo Daciano has returned to his favorite pastime."

"Are you insinuating that I'm *predictable?*" Mirceo sniffed. "How unsexy." Did he concern himself about nothing?

Cas warned the newcomers, "You do not want to challenge me tonight."

"We have no fight with you, demon." The leader pointed his sword at Mirceo. "We only want the vampire."

Cas's horns straightened, his fangs lengthening. *Only want the vampire?* His demonic instincts erupted to a savage degree. These six would try to kill Cas, then incapacitate Mirceo to take him alive. *Not while I've a breath. I'll slaughter them all.*

With a cocky lift of his brow, Mirceo said, "What would you want with little ol' me?"

"You are going to show us the way to Dacia."

"I certainly shall, lamb." Mirceo's own fangs and claws sharpened, his eyes turning black. "All you have to do is come and get me."

THIRTEEN

The Forbearers split up, three attacking the demon, the others targeting Mirceo.

The largest of that trio lunged for Mirceo, swinging his sword. Ducking under the whistling blade, Mirceo used his speed to maneuver around the other two.

He punched one in the back, cracking the male's spine and catching his weapon before it hit the ground. Severing the Forbearer's head, he faced off against the remaining pair. One brashly charged, telegraphing his moves; Mirceo coldly cut him down. Sword raised against the last of his trio, he chanced a glance at Caspion.

Blood sprayed half of the demon's face as he tore his second victim's head off. Caspion seized that vampire's sword, then used the decapitated body to block the last of those three Forbearers.

The demon's eyes were obsidian black, his muscles bulging, his sinews like whipcords.

My gods, look at him. Mirceo stared in awe. *He's as magnificent as I am.*

Caspion showed even more confidence and daring than before—and a thousand times more ferocity. *Because these enemies threatened his mate?*

The idea gave Mirceo a delicious rush of adrenaline—

"Look out!" Caspion yelled.

Mirceo traced, eluding a sword strike, then swung for his attacker's neck. Wet warmth spattered his chin as a head went flying and the body collapsed to the ground. Mirceo's opponents were finished, but the demon had one left.

Out of the corner of his eye, he spied Caspion pivot sideways as if to throw something. With a bloodcurdling roar, he flung his sword, sending it tumbling end-over-end in the air.

Right at me.

The weapon zoomed past Mirceo's head, slicing a lock of his hair. He twisted around.

Thunk. The blade had sunk into the eye of another Forbearer who'd just materialized behind Mirceo, weapon raised for a blow. The swordsman must have remained hidden, awaiting his moment.

Mirceo swung for the male's neck, and the headless body dropped. *Fuck me, that was close.*

He glanced over at Caspion. Without a sword—the demon had sacrificed it to protect Mirceo—Caspion used his horns to impale the last Forbearer.

Then the demon descended upon the male in a blur of fangs and claws. When Caspion finally pulled back, the decapitated corpse collapsed at his feet. Almost as an afterthought, Caspion tossed aside the severed head he was holding.

The demon scented the air for any other hidden dangers. Satisfied, he turned to Mirceo and swiped his sleeve over his mouth, smearing blood and sweat.

Mirceo's gut clenched with wanting.

Heaving breaths, they stared at each other. Mirceo cast about for something to say. *I desire you beyond reason, demon.* No, too heavy. *Say something cavalier.* "Bravo, sweetheart." He discarded his appropriated sword. "More deaths to add to your tally, making you even stronger."

Caspion was before him in an instant, his hand wrapped around Mirceo's throat. The demon lifted him by the neck high in the air. "You think I need more strength? I slew more foes in Poly than you ever will in your life, leechling."

Mirceo gasped, "Fair point."

Caspion wasn't done. "In the future, you dispatch your gods-damned enemies immediately. Understand me? You don't *play* with them. On second thought, you trace away to begin with."

Aww, he was worried about me. Mirceo couldn't breathe; his lips still curved into a grin.

"Why do I bother explaining things to you?" Caspion hurled him away, but Mirceo traced to right himself and landed on his feet.

When the demon snagged a flask from his coat pocket, Mirceo recognized the scent of demon brew. Not the cheap stuff either. Had Caspion truly amassed wealth over these centuries?

Pity. Mirceo had loved spoiling the demon. Rubbing his neck, he rasped, "In the past, you never expected me to trace away then, even told me I was an uncanny fighter." Mina wasn't the only talented swordsperson in the family. All Dacians were skilled with weaponry, but Mirceo had become an expert just to keep up with her. "So what's changed? Perhaps you were worried about *your mate?*"

"You are not my mate!" Another slug from his flask.

"How do you explain your concern? I might not be as strong as you are, demon, but I am a Dacian; I can handle myself."

"Then why did I have to yell for you to watch your back? What if I hadn't been here to warn you?"

"It was *your* fault I got distracted." Mirceo's gaze roamed over him. "I was entranced by my male. Your fighting style is different than it used to be."

"Happened over time. What of it?"

"You were also more aggressive—because your instincts were screaming for you to *protect me*."

~

Damn him for being right. Fear for Mirceo had *rocked* him. When that hidden Forbearer had appeared behind him . . .

"But you'll grow accustomed to those instincts with time, and we'll continue being a phenomenal team." Mirceo gestured at the carnage. "Look around us, demon. We could have a good run at this."

"At what?"

"Life together. And all that." Eyes lively, he said, "Let's spend the rest of eternity fighting and fucking."

"Did it ever occur to you that I might want more from life than that? I've long yearned for offspring. If I accept you as mine, I'll be relinquishing that hope forever."

Mirceo blinked at him.

"Self-centered leech! You never even considered that aspect?"

"I'm thirty; I consider very little in general." At Cas's disgusted look, Mirceo rolled his eyes. "Some of us aren't abruptly five centuries older."

"You know I want a family of my own. I talked of it often enough. *A line to come after me?* Ringing a bell? This was only weeks ago for you!"

"I just thought you'd . . . get over that idea. Together we'd find other interests."

"Amazing. Other bloody interests? Fucking and fighting?"

With a mulish look, the vampire said, "Maybe."

"You consider no one besides yourself! How did I ever become friends with you? You're nothing but a selfish player with no thoughts of the future. . . ." He trailed off as Mirceo spat repeatedly. "Are you even listening to me?"

"I accidentally tasted another's blood. It's foul!"

Cas gave a mocking laugh. "You're getting spoiled on mine. Which will hurt you all the more when I deprive you of it."

Mirceo scrubbed a palm over his mouth. "You would withhold it—when depriving me of lifeblood deprives you of pleasure?"

Cas had no argument for that; ceding blood was . . . ecstasy. The healing puncture wounds in his neck felt empty—as if his skin ached to be pierced once more. *To be filled.* "If I'd never experienced bloodtaking, then I wouldn't know about its effect. But you forced your bite on me!"

"I admit that wasn't my best moment." Mirceo shoved his long hair off his face. "I was in the grip of my blooding."

Again, Cas marveled at the timing. He'd never heard of a male so young finding his mate. "You drank from my flesh—will you dream of my past?" As a starving little guttersnipe named Beggar.

Back then, he'd had just enough pride to be blistered by shame hour after hour.

Cas remembered a vow he'd made to himself as a seven-year-old pup: *One day, when I never have to wear rags or beg anymore, I'll give myself a new name, a proud name.*

He had. He'd succeeded and kept that promise. But he could never erase what came before. . . .

The bite of snow against his bare feet. The hovel he'd called home. The unrelenting hunger. The cruelty of others: *If you want this feast, Beggar, you have to eat it with a little spice.*

Would Mirceo see Cas as a pup, sobbing on his hands and knees?

"I probably will," Mirceo said. "Since I tapped right into one of your firm, warm veins."

"You had no right!" Inhaling for calm, he said, "I thought the great Dacians didn't drink from the flesh."

"We didn't, until we installed Lothaire as king. He's very . . . progressive. Our entire kingdom's changing dramatically."

"How many others have you drunk besides me?" Cas grew nauseated at the idea of Mirceo sinking those fangs into someone else.

"No one. I will drink from my mate alone."

"Ah, for your mate, you'll keep your fangs in your mouth. But would you keep your dick in your pants?"

He squared his shoulders. "Yes."

"How long would that last before you got bored and strayed? You always have. You dreaded the mere prospect of being faithful to your mate."

"If I'd suspected I would have a mate like you, I would've rushed headlong."

Silver-tongued vampire. "In our first conversation, you described monogamy as *an intolerable hardship*. Remember when you likened it to stalking a boar that had already been felled?" He pinned Mirceo's gaze. "You forget—I *know* you."

"Is that the reason for your hesitation with me? Or is it because I'm male?"

Cas pinched the bridge of his nose. "You'd like it to be that simplistic, wouldn't you? Then you could assign all the blame to me, instead of having to look at your own failings. Have you ever considered that the problem lies with *you* specifically? Maybe I don't object to the fact that you have a cock. Maybe I object to the fact that your cock has you."

Mirceo scowled. "What the hell does that mean?"

"I'm an older demon, set in my ways, but I *can* evolve. If my dream mate came in this physical package"—he waved at Mirceo from head to toe—"I would happily embrace my destiny. But you're *not* my dream. You never will be. The sooner you realize that, the more pain you'll spare yourself."

"Dreams can change. I know this as well as anyone. In time, I'll convince you."

"In time?" Cas narrowed his gaze. "How do you keep finding me?"

"I figured you would return to this palace. But just in case, I have Trehan's scry talisman." Mirceo pulled a faceted crystal from his pants pocket, displaying it. "This has been passed down through his line—the House of Shadow—for generations. It's how he found you in Abaddon."

The crystal held Cas's gaze rapt.

"When I couldn't locate you for weeks, my uncle entrusted the priceless crystal to me, because he knows how important you are to me. He feels bad about the way he treated you. Do recall that he was under the influence of poison when you two faced off."

If not for that crystal, Trehan never would've found Abaddon or entered the tournament. Cas could've won, marrying his friend and remaining beloved by his people. He would be king of the very dimension that had scorned him.

Instead, he'd returned from five centuries of hell just in time for a spoiled, dissolute princeling to stalk him—using the same fucking crystal!

Cas's hand shot forward to snatch it. *Bane of my entire*

godsdamned existence! Baring his fangs, he squeezed his fist with all the new strength in his body.

Before Mirceo's disbelieving eyes, Cas crushed the thing—crushed it, then released the glittering dust on the night breeze. "Try finding me now." He teleported away.

~

Abandoned among the Forbearer remains, Mirceo punted a severed head. Damn it! Somehow he'd lost ground with his mate—and he'd lost the scry crystal forever.

How would he locate Caspion now? Luckily, Mirceo was a genius and would come up with a solution. Soon.

Until then, what would he do? Just as Mina had said, Caspion had *other* reservations about Mirceo. He exhaled a gust of breath. *Evolving as a person?* There had to be another way. . . .

Aha! Galvanized by an idea, he traced back to Dacia, to a laboratory deep within the bowels of the castle.

A large hearth fire illuminated workbenches covered with arcane magic supplies. Beakers wafted yellow smoke. Dried animal parts and bundles of herbs dangled from racks.

Mirceo glanced around, but spied no one. "Balery! Where are you? I need your help!"

A comely, pointed-eared fey emerged from a back room with her dark hair knotted atop her head. "What is it now?" She wiped her hands on a work apron, leaving smears of green slime. "You're worse than Lothaire with the yelling." Balery was a concoctioness and oracle; her ever-present pouch of seer bones was affixed to her belt.

The bones that told me of my mate. "This is urgent! My demon wants pups. I don't suppose you or someone you know could turn me female for a year?"

She rolled her doe-brown eyes. "There are easier ways to go about this, vampire."

"How? Tell me." He quelled the urge to grab her hands; Balery had poisonous skin. "Please."

"You'll need an egg."

"Yes! An egg." Pause. "What do I do with an egg?" Mirceo squinted with suspicion. "What *kind* of egg?"

Peering at the ceiling, she muttered, "Males." She looked at him again. "You'll need a vampire or demon egg. Or any species, really. Though not a giant's. *Food costs*," she added knowingly.

"Say I can get one. What then?"

"With a little of my magic, the demon's seed or yours—or a splice—will fertilize the egg. Then you'll be ready for the next step: finding a female to carry your bundle of joy."

A female? Mina would do it! Females loved having babies all the time.

"After a species-specific gestation period, you and your mate will have offspring."

"Have you done this before?"

"Of course." She made a scoffing sound. "You really are a young thirty, prince."

He sighed. "So I'm coming to believe."

"Some fated pairings require an extra step to reproduce. You and your mate aren't the first, and you won't be the last."

Mirceo pictured himself and Caspion as parents to a toddling pup and grinned. What possibility! "This sounds perfect. I would like to throw gold at this problem and delegate all parts of it." He waved his hand grandly.

Her eyes went wide. "Out of my lab, Mirceo! OUT!"

"Wait, wait! I was jesting. Mostly. In all seriousness, I will move mountains to give my mate whatever he needs. So how do I get an egg?"

"I should have a few around here somewhere." She opened and closed a couple of drawers.

"I don't need one *just* yet. He still has his seal." And without the crystal, Mirceo couldn't even find Caspion to tell him this good news. Ah, but Mirceo knew the demon's interests. He would track the tracker.

You can teleport, mate, but you can't hide.

"His seal?" Balery said. "I can't help you with *that*. Come talk to me when you wear your demon's mark."

Once Caspion claimed Mirceo, he would bite his neck, leaving his demonic mark forever. *Soon.* "I will. Thank you, Balery!" He blew her a kiss. Then he traced to Mina's suites, calling, "Sister, I need a *tiny* favor."

FOURTEEN

Going insane . . . For the last four days, Cas hadn't been able to focus on anything.

Sitting on the bed in his beach hideout, he squeezed his head in his hands. He felt as if he were back in Poly, enduring the hellishly slow passage of hours.

He'd tried to lose himself in reading, but he couldn't concentrate. He kept expecting Mirceo to show up here, though that was impossible now. No one knew about Cas's remote bungalow in the Hidden Seas, and Mirceo had no crystal.

Why had Cas destroyed it instead of stealing the thing? How idiotic and out of control!

Perhaps his demonic aggression was already cranked up—because he'd refused to claim his fated one.

No, fight this. Mirceo might have found his mate in Cas, yet that didn't mean the opposite was true.

So why did Cas feel like his guts were in knots?

He reached for a bottle of brew on the nightstand. Pulling the cork out with his teeth, he guzzled the liquid, but nothing could erase the memory of Mirceo's luscious seed on his lips.

The taste had seared Cas's mind and fueled unwanted thoughts ever since. *That seed is for* me *alone.* Even now, his claws sharpened, his horns straightening. He'd blooded Mirceo, bringing him back to life. *The vampire's body belongs to me.*

Fight this. Cas had considered availing himself of a courtesan—or five—but Mirceo's words continued to echo in his head: *Every time you're inside a female, I vow to the Lore I will be too. . . . I will let* males *take* me.

What if the leech was actually keeping his dick in his pants? If he heard about Cas's escapades, Mirceo would be compelled to comply with the terms of that ridiculous vow.

How could Cas enjoy fucking anyone when it could result in some other male fucking Mirceo?

Jealousy scored him. He shot to his feet and rammed his aching horns into the wall, adding new holes to go with the other ones peppering the room. "Should kill him for this!" That vampire had him so twisted up inside.

Sensual, laughing Mirceo. With his mocking gray eyes and devil-may-care attitude.

Cas rubbed the heel of his palm down his hard shaft. His skin felt tight all over, his limbs heavy. Realization hit him: Mirceo's two feedings had set off changes in Cas's body, prompting it to produce more blood—to adapt to a vampire's hungers. Cas's veins were brimming. Such an excess meant his cock remained stiff as a titanium rod.

I'm a fucking host. Another outcome he'd had no control over! With a yell, he punched the wall, adding yet another hole.

Claustrophobia surged, his throat tightening. *Need a job. Anything to distract me.* Cas snatched on a coat and his sword belt, then traced to the Red Flag, a tavern in New Orleans that catered to bounty hunters. He recognized several of those inside.

A group of lion shifters and a berserker played dice in the back. A few smoke demons relaxed in front of the fire.

On the way to the bar, Cas passed an extended wall covered with bounty postings. Whenever someone offered a reward anywhere in the Lore, a copy would mystically appear here and at other similar establishments. If a hunter took down a poster, it disappeared from all locations, and he was bound to complete the task, upon penalty of death.

Varying in terms of payout and difficulty, the jobs ranged from something as simple as finding an inanimate object to the most extreme—apprehending a sorcerer from his impenetrable fortress on Poly.

Before Cas left here tonight, he would select a challenging hunt—but not too challenging, not until he got his mind in order.

Taking a seat at the bar, he recalled his start in this business, the fateful MISSING poster he'd come across when he was twelve. He hadn't been able to make out the words, but he'd overheard some other kids reading it aloud. A nobledemon had lost his miniature hellhound, a stray Cas had noticed sniffing around the slums.

Easy enough. Cas had delivered the hellhound to its owner, collecting more money than he'd ever seen. He'd discovered he had a talent for finding lost mementos and pets. In two years, he'd grown such a reputation—his name of *Beggar* replaced by *Tracker*—that other hunters had traced him to this tavern, to the "big leagues." *Bounty hunting. . . .*

Now the tavern's grizzled demon barkeep shuffled over. "Been wondering when you'd show." Leyak, a retired hunter and Cas's de facto mentor, was as much a fixture in this place as the wall of postings. "Brew, son?" Unlike most immortals, the gray-haired

Leyak continued to slowly age past his prime, his face weathered and horns scuffed. He must have a human ancestor somewhere in his line.

"Always." When Leyak poured an expensive vintage, Cas said, "Are we celebrating something?"

The demon rolled his eyes. "I figure you got gold aplenty now."

"How's that?"

"Almost every bounty posting connected to Poly disappeared from that wall in seconds. I suspected you were raking it in."

True. Lorean dregs often hid out in that dimension. A squalid hunter's bar there had provided Cas with new notices. Like a spider on a web, he'd collected them one by one.

"Nothing gets past you." All those years ago, the eagle-eyed hunter had realized Cas couldn't read the posters. Instead of ridiculing him, Leyak had read several aloud, as if commenting on them, never letting the other hunters know.

Leyak had been the only one who'd believed a fourteen-year-old like Cas could collect on the first live bounty he'd chosen. Afterward, the old demon had said, "You stalked that trail like a Caspion tiger, son!"

Cas had liked the name, and so he'd claimed it. . . .

"Surely you're not looking for a job," Leyak said now. "See, son, when folks make a heap of money, they do this thing called *retiring*."

"Trying to keep busy." Cas sampled his drink, his thoughts returning to Mirceo. What if additional Forbearers stalked the vampire? Mirceo traveled outside Dacia more than any others in that family—aside from Trehan, who was far too powerful for turned humans to challenge.

The Forbearers had known where to look for Mirceo. Their order would send out another force. And another one. Mirceo would never be safe. What if he'd already been captured?

Could I ever find him? Cas's instinct to hunt burned—

"A fellow mentioned you by name last night," Leyak said. "A vampire."

Cas cursed the surge of excitement that the demon's words roused. "Oh?"

"A clear-eyed one. Quite charming for a leech."

Did Mirceo plan to infiltrate all parts of his life? When Cas's claws shot even longer, he sank them into his palms. The bite of pain made him ache for the vampire to feed, to empty him of all this excess blood. "Can't say this is a surprise. He's been searching for me."

Leyak blinked. "He didn't ask after your whereabouts. Just used your name to get in the door here."

A chill swept over Cas. "Are you saying he took a job?"

Leyak's gaze shifted to the poster wall, where one ancient notice was conspicuously absent. "I'm saying he took *the* job."

FIFTEEN

W*hat the hell, vampire?"* The demon shoved Mirceo outside of the Red Flag a nanosecond after he'd arrived.

"Is there a problem, sweetheart?" Mirceo had made sure enough of these hunters knew he was returning tonight.

Caspion released him. "You have no idea what you've done!"

Mirceo adjusted his trench coat. "You look tense." An understatement.

The demon's muscles were knotted, his teeth gritted. His member was semihard and growing. "Tense? *Tense???*"

"Indeed." But Caspion's face was weary. *These four days apart haven't been difficult for me alone.* Mirceo had been choking down cups of non-Caspion blood just to maintain his weight. At his young age, a missed feeding hit hard. "If you'd like to take a moment to compose yourself, I have business to attend to inside."

Caspion cast him a mystified look. "You're not going anywhere."

"Am I not?"

"Did you know you are obligated to complete any bounty you take from that wall? If you fail, the other hunters will all come after you. To *kill* you."

"Someone might've alluded to that." *After* Mirceo had yanked down the parchment. *Funny, gentlemen, realllll funny.*

Caspion scrubbed his hand over his face. "How did you even know to come to this tavern?"

"You mentioned it once." He'd described it as a meeting place and exchange for hunters. Since Mirceo had possessed zero alternatives for finding Caspion, he'd laid a trap of his own.

"Let's see the job." The demon snapped his fingers. "Now."

"No need to be a churlish lout." Mirceo pulled the poster from his trench, unfolding it. "Allow me to read it for—"

Caspion snatched the parchment. "I can read now."

"My brilliant mate." Caspion did a double-take at Mirceo's sudden smile. "You fill me with pride. I told you all those books would be read by you. Only I had thought to teach you."

Pulling at his collar, he said in a gruff tone, "Taught myself."

Mirceo sighed. "Haven't I always complimented you on your considerable intellect?"

The demon scowled. "Can we get back to this?" Then he read:

WANTED!
DEAD OR ALIVE
ADHAM "SILT" HAREA, THE SORCERI KING OF SAND
MURDERER, CANNIBAL, OATH BREAKER, INVOKER OF
DARK RITES, AND FUGITIVE FROM THE LAW
LAST SEEN: THE PLANE OF LOST YEARS
REWARD: FORTY DRAGON-GOLD COINS
OFFERED BY THE GAOLERS

Caspion's lips parted. "How could you have . . . why did you pick *this* one?"

It had looked like an ideal job with lots of money, which the demon had always been concerned about. At least in the past. "Because I'm keen to visit the Poly." To see where his mate had lived—*away from me*—for so long.

"Just *Poly*," Caspion corrected. "You don't know the first thing about tracking down a bounty."

"That's true. If only I had a scry crystal." He tapped his chin. "Oh, wait . . ."

"You deserved that and more."

Shrug. "Since you robbed me of the crystal's use, you should show me the ropes. We could split the huge payout on this one. Do you know how valuable dragon gold is?"

"I don't need money, leechling! I made plenty on Poly."

"Exactly—you know the terrain there."

"There's a reason this job still posted," Caspion said, sounding exasperated. "It is *impossible*."

"If we work together, I'm sure we can find a random sorcerer." Besides, Mirceo was chafing for the chance to prove himself to his mate.

"I can already *find* him. You think I spent centuries in that place unaware of the most coveted bounty in the realm?"

"Then why haven't you claimed it?"

"Did you even *read* the poster before you took it down?"

"Sure." He'd noted the reward and the location.

"That sorcerer's lair is protected both physically and mystically. No one can fight their way past the monsters guarding it, and sorcery prevents anyone from tracing past them."

Mirceo retrieved his flask of blood mead from his trench coat. "Explain."

"Harea's pyramid fortress lies in the center of an enormous valley that he's bespelled to prevent teleporting. Anyone who tries it will fail, then get swallowed by sand. That valley also happens to be where Wendigos congregate. Starving ones. There are hundreds of them."

Wendigos were like zombies, but lightning fast. Mirceo had heard stories of just one decimating whole settlements of immortals. "We can handle them. I'm a master swordsman, remember?"

"Just to get in striking range, you'd have to evade the Wendigos, then cross the wasteland of sand that surrounds the pyramid. That stretch is filled with gulgs—living quicksand traps."

"They sound dire. But we can scout the area, map out their locations, then avoid them."

"You could. Except gulgs *move* within their territory. They can scent their prey and attack it. Say you got past those alive—without teleporting a single time—you'd still have to face a mystical boundary around the fortress and the sand scyllas."

"Do I even want to know?"

"They're gigantic tentacle creatures that burrow under the pyramid. If a trespasser gets too close, their tentacles shoot to the surface, dragging the unwary down to be eaten. The hope is that you suffocate in the sand *before* the digestion starts."

Mirceo had heard of pleasanter scenarios. "I have a hard time believing this fortress is impenetrable. I come from an impenetrable realm." At least until Lothaire made good on his promise to open the doors wide. "With a target in sight, there are sorcerers and witches who could circumvent these security measures."

Cas shook his head. "Most of the ones who *could* get past the barriers *won't.*"

"Why?"

"Out of respect for their brethren's spells. Plus, those hex-hacks are likely to run into bounties on their own heads as well. None of them want to face the Gaolers."

"What's so scary about them?" Mirceo asked. "They sound like your typical Lorean gang."

"They're *demigod* wraiths who act as a type of Lore patrol. They quarantine contagious Loreans, capture any humans about to broadcast proof of our world, and dispatch evil immortals to lifelong torments."

"Contagious Loreans?"

Caspion nodded. "Plague-stricken vampires, ghouls, zombies. There's a reason why Wendigos haven't overrun the mortal plane."

"Where are these bounties taken?" Mirceo asked.

"No one knows for sure, but some whisper of an immortal prison."

Mirceo stiffened. "Mortals put my uncle in such a place." Even an ancient immortal like Lothaire had barely gotten out alive.

"This is supposed to be an entire *dimension*, but no one can confirm or deny its existence. Bottom line: The Gaolers are not the type of beings you *want* to come in contact with."

"I have no fear of facing them. I've done no evil. Well, not an *excessive* amount of evil." Mirceo shrugged. "You've outlined some considerable challenges to my bounty. More and more, this operation—or *op*, as we bounty hunters like to say—is beginning to sound like a heist. Fortunately for us, I am a vampire of many talents. Even *nonsexual ones*."

"You're not listening. . . ." Caspion pinched the bridge of his nose.

"How do you know so much about this?"

"Over the last five centuries, whenever I heard a hunter was going after Harea, I traced to edge of that valley to study the attempt. The Wendigos took out most. The gulgs got the rest.

Only one—a winged volar demon—neared the pyramid's mystical barrier. The scyllas snatched him down. These were all talented hunters, often men I knew. I watched them try, and I watched them die. And now you must participate in this hunt or you'll be killed!" He stabbed his fingers through his tousled hair. "Mirceo, I can't simply *fix* this for you."

"So either way I'm damned?"

Caspion rasped, *"Yes."*

"There, there." He patted the demon's shoulder. "If I'm on borrowed time, we should get going. One last adventure!"

Caspion's eyes widened. "You impulsive, rash child, are you eager to die?"

"I *did* put some thought into this." At the demon's disbelieving look, he said, "I plan to float right past all the security protocols. The only danger would be in dying from boredom."

"Arrogant leechling. What are you talking about?"

"Would a sorcerer have the foresight to protect against the abilities of a 'mythical' species? Dacians can turn themselves into mist. Now that you've blooded me, I can turn you as well."

Caspion's lips parted on a breath.

Mirceo grinned at his reaction. "Not such an impulsive leechling after all, am I?"

Recovering from his surprise, he said, "If you lost your focus like you did in that Forbearer skirmish, you'd be dead. I won't always be able to protect you."

Mirceo squared his shoulders. "I'll hold my own, demon. You forget, I'm not asking you for permission. I am inviting you—on *my* op. Perhaps I should invite another hunter?" He turned toward the entrance of the tavern.

Making a sound of frustration, the demon traced in front of him. "Even if we somehow breached the fortress, we'd still have to subdue the sorcerer, and Harea is not just some random Poly warlord. I have mystical restraints that will dampen his magic, but until we shackle him, we're at risk."

"What powers does he possess?"

"He's the Sorceri King of Sand, which means he controls every grain of it. Trust me when I say he's got a lot of ammunition on Poly. And he's ancient—some say his sorcery created the great pyramids."

"He sounds like a heavy-hitter. Luckily, we are as well. You're a five-century-old death demon who's racked up a legion of kills, and I'm a Dacian, which is enough said. We are going to be unstoppable."

"You're truly serious about this." Exhaling a long breath, Caspion said, "Fine. I'll help you, saving your ass yet again."

Part of him was shocked that Caspion had agreed. "Excellent."

Pointing his forefinger at Mirceo's face, the demon said, "You do not speak to anyone there. Do not look at anyone. Do not touch *anything.*"

"Yes, sir!" Mirceo said, fighting a smile. "Any other commands?"

"Yeah. Put on a fucking shirt."

SIXTEEN

The winds in Poly could scour skin down to the bone. Mirceo's bared chest wasn't going to cut it.

Once the vampire had returned from donning a form-fitting black shirt, he flashed Cas his rakish grin. "Do I pass muster?" he asked, all too aware of his sex appeal.

Cas had seen him wield it like a weapon. "You'll do," he said dismissively, though his cock had stirred from just that grin. "It's impossible to predict Poly's day and night from this realm. We could be heading into noonday sun, so I'll trace you to a shelter first." The few bars there were filled with deadly beings—who could prove just as lethal to Mirceo as the sun—so Cas would have to take him to his former home. "We might have to wait it out."

More waiting on Poly? Just when Cas had thought he was free of that hellhole, he got sucked back in.

Were they actually going to do this? Wasn't like they had a choice. For a male who revered options, Cas had none—because

Mirceo had behaved with such recklessness. Expected, considering his age.

Did Cas want that bounty? Of course. But he also recalled how he'd felt watching Mirceo fight. *So much risk.* Exhaling with resignation, he gripped the vampire's arm, then teleported him to an isolated cave in the northern mountains of Poly.

Cas released him and crossed the dark toward a lantern. As light chased away the gloom, he tried to see the place through Mirceo's eyes.

The area was spartan and organized with military precision. Trunks of weapons and gear lined one wall. Peat logs lined another. The bed consisted of furs piled atop a raised shelf of rock. Beside the nearby fire pit, smoke stains stretched up to the cavern ceiling.

Outside, the winds howled, whipping the flap of canvas that served as a door. Caspion traced to the flap, peering out. "It's night, but not late enough." He returned to sit on a trunk. "We'll head out in an hour."

The vampire meandered through the cave. "Was this one of your camps?"

What insights into Cas's private life could a clever male like Mirceo gain from this visit? "You're looking at home sweet home."

"You lived in this dismal little cave *for centuries?*" The spoiled princeling's tone was aghast.

"Unlike you, I don't need much." Cas was used to little.

"Why did you leave gear here?" The vampire traced to one of the trunks, opening the lid.

"Always good to have a bolt hole."

Mirceo's eyes widened at the trunk's contents. "So many books." He flipped through a couple.

The vampire had promised Cas that he would read one day.

Cas had *believed* him, studying his ass off to learn. He could even read Demonish.

Would Mirceo notice that Cas had all the titles the prince had once read to him?

If so, Mirceo didn't remark on it, just closed the trunk. But his mood seemed lighter. "What did you eat?"

"Whatever I could hunt." Reptilian creatures, mostly.

"And females?" Mirceo dropped down on the sleeping pallet.

How many times had Cas imagined the vampire on those furs, there for his use? *For me to dominate and control.* To distract himself, he snagged some tinder and a couple of peat logs to build a fire. "Females were scarce." Cas's appetite for sex had grown in lockstep with his burgeoning strength, but he'd had few outlets for it. "I was in that outpost tavern for a reason."

Mirceo's lips thinned. "I didn't take you for such an ascetic."

"All things being equal, I enjoy comforts. But Poly affords few of them."

"You must've really wanted to stay away. From me."

"Not everything is about you, leechling." *But wasn't that a huge part of it?*

"Then tell me what was this penance was about."

"I wanted to get stronger and seek my fortunes." Before he'd left Abaddon, he'd vowed to Bettina: *I will do anything— anything—so that I may never know defeat like that again.* "I promised myself I would stay until I'd accumulated a certain amount of wealth and kills. Those goals took me five centuries to achieve."

Glancing to the right of Cas, Mirceo asked, "Did you think of me?"

Some minutes less than others. "Perhaps on occasion." Cas

hadn't comprehended how much he would crave the simple *companionship* of their relationship until he'd lost it. Always, he'd missed his best friend.

But at night, alone in this cave, he'd found his thoughts turning . . . darker.

Aside from masturbating to the memory of their kiss, he'd conjured up filthy fantasies about Mirceo. Cas would stroke himself to a bone-melting release, yelling with equal parts pleasure and frustration.

He recalled the last one he'd indulged in here.

Cas unlacing his breeches and ordering Mirceo to suck . . . the prince's gray eyes dancing as he dropped to his knees . . . using the vampire's hot mouth . . . giving Mirceo his cum . . . the vampire taking his due and biting Cas's cock. . . .

That fantasy had made him culminate so hard his back had bowed.

Cas tugged his coat down to conceal his raging hard-on. *Gods almighty. Filthy.*

"Only on occasion, demon?" Mirceo's words ripped Cas from his memories. "At least one of us can lie. I'll bet you thought of me and fondled your mouthwatering member on these very furs." Mirceo skimmed his fingers through the top one, his pale vampire skin stark against silken black.

Mercy. Those deft fingers had encircled Cas's shaft mere nights ago, forcing it against Mirceo's own. That semen-slicked clutch . . .

"How long will you deny I'm yours?" Mirceo asked. "You saw your pre-cum. You know it's for me."

"And *why* would I produce pre-cum? I can't impregnate you."

Irritation flashed in the vampire's expression. "Is spawning all sex is good for? Because that was the last thing you were thinking about when you tagged every available female across the worlds.

Besides, you're to give me seed because it will bond us. Just as sharing blood does."

The more Cas struggled *not* to imagine coming inside Mirceo, the more vivid the image grew. Frustration simmered. "So I should accept having no offspring without even a qualm?"

"You can't impregnate anyone until you break your seal, and you can't do that without me. In any case, I've found a way for us to have children, even with me as your mate. But you'll probably be too stubborn to listen."

"Tell me how that would be possible."

"We would use a donated egg for you—or us—to fertilize. Mina said she'd happily carry a babe for us."

"So not only would she be trapped down there in Dacia, she'd be trapped *and* pregnant."

He stiffened. "She's not *trapped.*"

"Uh-huh. You can't keep her shut away forever."

Mirceo's eyes flickered black with emotion. "*Watch me.* I will lock her in Dacia's dungeon before she ever leaves the protection of the realm."

Cas raised his brows.

Mirceo released a breath. "It's a sore subject. Lothaire has been hinting around about sending her into the otherlands for *education.* If she stayed in her mist, she should be safe from the plague, but so many things could go wrong. If she lost concentration or grew too exhausted . . . or if Forbearers somehow found her . . ." He looked as if he were imagining every worst-case scenario. At length, he said, "I'll take Lothaire's godsdamned head before he sends her away."

All the best with that, you rash young leechling. Lothaire was rumored to be one of the longest-lived vampires in existence— which meant he would be diabolically powerful.

Canting his head, Mirceo said, "You feel protective of Mina already, don't you?" *I . . . do.* "You can scorn me all you want, but you are her brother-by-fate now. And she's thrilled to be your sister. Your family just got bigger."

"Silver-tongued as ever," Cas said in an indifferent tone, but the vampire had gotten him thinking. "Where would the egg come from?"

"Balery, my uncle's concoctioness and oracle, has some."

"You expect me to trust a seeress—who serves the Enemy of Old—to engineer a pup of mine?"

"Yes. Because I trust her."

"And would *you* be my partner in parenting?" Cas scoffed. "May the gods help any younglings with you as a father."

"Staked through the heart, demon." All light left Mirceo's eyes, and Cas wanted it back. "No one has ever wounded me like you do."

Mirceo had always struck him as unflappable, his emotions bulletproof. Did the vampire's uncaring façade hide a more sensitive self?

"Before I met you, I never thought about bringing children into the worlds," Mirceo said, holding Cas's gaze, "but the idea of creating something with you, then protecting it, appeals deeply to me. It would be a worthwhile endeavor, no? A fulfilling one?"

The vampire's words surprised him. What if Mirceo could somehow stay true and committed to a shared future?

"How long would that occupy you before you grew bored? I saw you burn through scores of partners. You simply aren't capable of eternity, and I'd accept nothing less from my mate."

"You've a lot of nerve to call me out on the number of partners. The notches on your belt must be infinite."

"Yes, but I made sure my bedmates weren't looking for more.

Not usually a problem, since I was an impoverished demon of zero import. But with a rich prince like you, well, people start to dream. Every soul you've bedded ached for more of you, but you would cast them that look—"

"What look?"

"The *it's-been-swell* look. The one that said you wanted nothing more to do with them." Cas could see himself among that number, ruined forever by the vampire's incomparable sex appeal. *What if I start to dream?* "Your eye was always on the next conquest."

"Just as you've changed, so have I." Mirceo sounded confident. "I am ready for this. Only your stubbornness holds us back."

"You're the youngest mated male I've heard of in all my years. But finding your mate early is not a good thing. There's a reason most immortals go centuries before facing that kind of commitment—because they are in no way prepared to handle it when young."

"Damn you, demon, I don't *want* others!" Mirceo's elegant fingers gripped the furs—another visual to torment Cas for eons. "I don't desire or need them." The vampire couldn't lie, so he'd meant what he said. For now. In the future, the prince's outlook would change. "We could grow the House of Castellan together."

"I listened to you about journeying to Dacia, because you'd all but beguiled me by that point. Now I wonder what in the hell I'd been thinking. Would I—the spawn of a nameless death demon, with no ancestral line to speak of—be welcome inside those hallowed Dacian halls? If you actually believe that, you're kidding yourself." Just one more reason the two of them would never work. Cas rose and paced, restless in the suddenly too-small cave.

Brows drawn, Mirceo watched him. "I am trying, Caspion. I want only to be what you need."

"You can't force these things. Sometimes you have to let things just . . . be."

"Easier said . . ."

He needed Mirceo to listen to him. "Here, in the grueling downtime between hunts, I would *will* time to pass faster." He'd lain on those furs, memorizing every nuance of the cave ceiling, his mind turning. Hell, Cas had welcomed the surprise whenever a stray Wendigo wandered past the flap. "No endeavor in the worlds could madden a demon so much as that. I finally learned to let go. I simply had to take the pain and accept my lot."

"I'll never accept a life without you in it," Mirceo said. "You're denying us for reasons that no longer apply. Why? Perhaps you don't lack faith in *me*. Perhaps you lack faith in *you*."

"What does that mean?"

"Chew it over. We'll discuss it after we collect our *impossible* bounty." Mirceo removed his sword belt and his trench coat, tossing them atop a trunk.

Cas cleared his throat. "What are you doing?"

"Settling in for the duration." He reclined on the furs, hands behind his head.

The vampire in my bed. Desire was a whip across Cas's back.

"If only we had something to do to kill time." Mirceo's voice was lazy, seductive. That sexual tension sizzled between them. "I could use a top-off, and you look like you're about to burst."

"Because you're turning me into a host!" Cas could bloodlet, but that would help for only so long. Whenever a host lost blood, his body assumed he was ceding it to a vampire, so it would produce an excess.

And right now, Cas's excess had settled into his groin—away from his brain. How was he going to concentrate on the job like this? He needed to drain himself of blood—and *pressure*.

Holding Cas's gaze, Mirceo murmured, "Won't you feed me, Caspion? I'll make it good for you."

Finally Mirceo had *asked*. Who could deny this prince? "Fine. You'll have your dinner from me. But we'll do it *my* way." Mirceo had manipulated Cas; why not use the vampire to make one of his countless fantasies come true?

Expression brightening, Mirceo traced to stand before him. "What did you have in mind?"

"I'm going to show you what I'd expect from my mate." *Reclaim control. Dominate the prince.* "And, leechling . . . you are not going to like it."

SEVENTEEN

Caspion eased ever closer. His swollen horns were straightened, his eyes gone black. Even his fangs had lengthened. *So wickedly demonic.* "I'm going to own you for a time. Because that is what I do to my partners." At Mirceo's ear, he rasped, "I'm going to own you because you're a prince, and I think a part of me hates you for that. A part of me needs to put you on your knees."

These dark musings got Mirceo harder than he'd ever been. Pre-cum wet the inside of his breeches.

He reached for Caspion's shaft, but the demon seized his wrist. "Ah-ah. I'm in control. Take off my sword."

With an intrigued lift of his brows, Mirceo unbuckled Caspion's weathered sword belt, then tossed it away.

In reward, the demon used a black claw to cut a line along his own neck. "Come, have a taste."

Mirceo eagerly did, leaning in to daub his tongue. A moan escaped his lips.

"My blood rules you, doesn't it?"

If this was Caspion's idea to scare Mirceo away . . . failure was at hand for the demon. "There is nothing like it."

"And biting me?"

"When your flesh gloves my fangs, I see heaven."

Caspion swallowed thickly. "Unbutton my shirt."

Mirceo did, spreading the material wide to bare the demon's brawny torso. Blond chest hair glinted in the firelight. *I've wanted to nuzzle it since I first met him.* Mirceo was helpless not to now, rubbing his face in it, inhaling with delight.

Caspion hissed in a breath, then sliced a line above his nipple. "Suck, vampire."

Mirceo eased over to press his mouth to the crimson. As he sucked, his tongue teased the hard little point, eliciting a growl from the demon.

Caspion cut a line above his other nipple, drawing Mirceo to it as well. Repeating his suck, Mirceo grew nigh dizzy on the luscious wine offered to him.

"What would you do for my blood?" Caspion demanded, voice a low rumble.

Dazed, Mirceo whispered, "Anything."

"You'd plead for it—just as you'd plead for me to fuck you. To give you my claiming bite."

The idea of Caspion marking him got Mirceo even harder. "I'll plead, if that's what it takes. I need to be possessed by you." He didn't necessarily crave penetration, but he would make the most of it to have Caspion. Maybe Mirceo could eventually persuade him into receiving on occasion. "It's just a matter of time, demon." The longer Caspion waited, the more out of control he would grow. "Fate will only let you resist for so long."

Clasping Mirceo's nape, Caspion leaned down. "Shut up." His firm lips took Mirceo's, his pointed tongue seeking.

Mirceo met him, groaning into the kiss. The demon had to be able to taste the blood, but it didn't cool his ardor. Caspion's aggression was palpable—and mounting. He deepened the contact, owning this kiss until Mirceo's knees went weak.

He dug his claws into the demon's broad shoulders. Though Mirceo was a formidable Dacian, he felt like ivy clinging to an oak.

Just when he surrendered completely, the demon broke away. "Got me all twisted!" Caspion reached down to untie his pants. "I know better than to want you." He shoved the leather down his thighs.

Mirceo had to clear his throat to speak. "But I was born for . . ." He trailed off, scenting a new source of blood.

Caspion pinched his chin, forcing him to look down. From a patch of silky blond curls, the demon's thick rod strained toward Mirceo, as if offering itself up for a bite.

A narrow slice graced the length. Gods almighty! Would Caspion make him drink from his shaft?

Make me, Mirceo inwardly begged. *Ah, for the love of gods, make me.* He stared at his mate's member, rapt, as blood pulsed along prominent veins and beaded atop that cut. The broad head was rose red, engorged with ever more blood.

I've never beheld anything so perfect. To feed from that font . . . ? Mirceo's fangs throbbed.

Increasing the pressure on Mirceo's head, Caspion said, "To your knees, princeling."

~

Lust seething in his gray eyes, Mirceo dropped down. Cas had expected he'd go straightaway for the blood, but the vampire took his time.

Though Cas was in control, Mirceo wasn't cowed. Smirking up at him, the prince rubbed his chiseled face against the other side of Cas's shaft.

Gone dizzy with bliss, Cas choked out words: "Have you . . . ever sucked a cock before?"

Mirceo shook his head. "But fear not; I excel at my every endeavor."

Cas thumped the arrogant vampire's ear.

Laughing, Mirceo dipped to nurse on Cas's balls.

"Fuck!" He bucked his hips for more.

With a grin, Mirceo tugged Cas's length down to lick pre-cum from the tip. But then the joke was on Mirceo, because the taste obviously slayed the prince. When Mirceo's eyes rolled back in his head, Cas thought he'd come spontaneously—

Groaning, the vampire engulfed Cas's shaft into the wet heat of his mouth. He clawed Cas's bare ass to drag him closer, flicking his clever tongue as he sucked.

Gripping Mirceo's head, Cas forced his cock even deeper, but the vampire kept moaning for more. No one had ever swallowed so much of him! "*Uhn!* Take all of me." Unable to stop himself, he thrust between Mirceo's lips, fucking the prince's mouth. Before Cas was ready, his balls drew up. Tremors climbed his spine, his toes curling.

Pulling back, Mirceo rasped, "Ah-ah. Not yet, lover." He ripped open his own pants as he dipped the tip of his tongue into the slit.

Cas could only stare in disbelief. "You're hungry for more?"

All blazing arrogance, Mirceo said, "Always. I *am* a spoiled prince." He sank his fangs into Cas's rigid flesh.

And the world spun.

EIGHTEEN

The demon's wine bathed his tongue. Struggling not to come from the sultry taste, Mirceo began to suck.

"Gods almighty!" Caspion groaned with pleasure. "Drink me. *Drink me down.*"

As Mirceo fed, he gazed up at this god of a male. Caspion was such a fierce warrior, an alpha to the core—but vulnerable. Despite kneeling at his feet, Mirceo still possessed power.

I'll have all of you. One day. . . .

For now, he lost himself in Caspion's lifeblood, his helpless reactions, his frenzied need. As the demon's rod throbbed around his fangs, Mirceo dared not touch his own member, lest he spill at once.

The demon cast him a brows-drawn, lost look. "I'm going to come right on your tongue, vampire."

Mirceo grasped Caspion's heavy balls, tugging on them, drawing a yell from the demon. More pre-cum arose to mix with the blood.

Delectable... Mirceo was finished. He couldn't withstand the pressure of his own seed ascending his shaft. He lowered a shaking hand, grasping himself.

A single jerk of his fist.

To the music of Caspion's moans, he began to spend between the demon's boots. As semen spurted across the sand, he snarled around Caspion's cock, planting his fangs even deeper.

The demon growled, "The scent of your cum maddens me!" He started to culminate, his shaft pulsating in Mirceo's hungry mouth. "You've ended me... *ENDED ME!*" He threw back his head and roared till the cave quaked around them.

~

With a loving lick, the vampire released his bite.

So much better than fantasy. Legs gone boneless, Cas stumbled back to his bed, sprawling on the furs. He grasped for his anger, wanting to stoke it, but all he felt was . . . peace. His body floated, euphoria drugging him.

Mirceo traced to lie beside him, resting his head on Cas's chest, his long black hair fanning out. Warm puffs of his breath breezed over Cas's dampened skin.

What if the prince is mine?

"Listen to that mighty heart beating," Mirceo murmured. "You can deny you love this all you want to, but your body tells a different story."

The vampire's intoxicating scent—sandalwood and a touch of blood—lit up Cas's mind. He shallowed his own breaths, just to take in more of that scent.

It was a tantalizing tease, with an undercurrent of fire—like Mirceo as a person.

Cas stared down at that long black hair. He'd gripped it before, but hadn't registered the feel of it. Could it be as soft as it looked? His fingers decided to find out, threading themselves through Mirceo's hair.

Soft like silk. Cas grew heavy-lidded with satisfaction. He gazed up at the nuances of the cave ceiling not with resignation and misery, but with a fragile hope kindling inside his chest.

He allowed himself a few moments to explore this afterplay. He'd always vaulted out of a partner's bed as soon as he'd come. Restless Mirceo had as well. Yet now the two of them lazed together.

Outside the winds howled. Inside the fire crackled. *I could lie like this forever.*

Reading his mind, Mirceo said, "This is almost as good as the release that got us here. Who knew?"

Who indeed? It was *too* good. "You always split well before the morning after."

"Depends on how drunk I got the night before. But to your point, I wasn't much of an afterglow kind of male. I always felt panic after sex. I don't know why."

Cas did. Because Mirceo was terrified of commitment. Fear doused Cas's hope, his instinct for self-preservation rising. This situation boiled down to a simple equation: *If I claim him as my own and he rejects me, then I'll be destroyed.*

More simply: *Mirceo equals doom.*

Cas shook his head hard. All of this agonizing would be moot if they didn't survive the next few hours. He needed to focus on their hunt, or he'd get them killed. "Up with you. We should talk some logistics."

Mirceo sighed. "Very well." He rose and adjusted his clothing. Tracing to sit on one of the trunks across from the bed, he secured his hair back with a leather tie.

Cas pulled his pants up over his still-swollen shaft. The mere glimpse of those fang marks nearly landed Mirceo back on the furs. *Focus!* "How long can you keep us in mist form?" He buttoned his shirt.

"By myself, indefinitely. With you, I don't know. Let's say half an hour."

"Then we should . . ." He trailed off, catching sight of the vampire's leavings on the floor of the cave. Pearlescent seed against opaque sand. Riveting—

Mirceo kicked more sand over it, burying it, breaking Cas's stare. Eyes merry, he said, "Had to, or else you'd never be able to concentrate—and some of us are professionals here."

Hating that the vampire was right, Cas struggled to concentrate. *Where were we?* Ah, half an hour. "That won't be enough time for us to cross the entire gulg valley. But I have an idea to get past them." Cas would turn a negative into a positive. He didn't explain his plan, and Mirceo apparently trusted him enough not to demand details.

"Do you think the sorcerer's guilty of all those things on the poster?"

Cas held up a palm. "Ah-ah. We don't *care.* Never concern yourself with any specifics other than who, when, where, and how much," he instructed, as if the prince was actually his new hunting partner.

"You aren't a touch curious about Harea?" Mirceo asked. "Or sympathetic? He sounds larger than life."

"Not at all. He's just a job."

"If the Gaolers are so imposing, why don't they go after the sorcerer themselves?"

"I don't know," Cas said. "Some say they can't enter all dimensions."

"They provided no contact information. How will we get paid?"

"I think they're keeping tabs on the sorcerer. The second Harea leaves Poly, they'll sense his new location. We'll take him behind the Red Flag and wait for them there." Cas traced to the flap again, glancing outside. "It's time." He turned back, snagging supplies from a trunk: a large tarp, mystical restraints, and two long rolls of cloth to cover their eyes and faces.

Mirceo donned his sword and his trench coat, then drew on a pair of gloves from his pocket. "Then let's be away."

"You can't go out like that. You need more protection." Cas tossed him a roll.

The vampire caught the cloth, blinking at him.

Cas unwound his own. "Watch me. It starts at your head. That will put this thin gauzy part over your eyes." He knotted the end around his neck.

"A little help here. I haven't had five centuries of practice with this."

Cas scowled. "Now I'm to dress you?"

"I'd much prefer the opposite, but yes, I'll need assistance. Whereas I mastered my blowjob technique on my first foray, I'd rather not risk my flawless face."

Muttering, "Arrogant leech," Cas traced to him and reached for the material.

Heat emanated from Mirceo, the young vampire as hot-blooded as ever.

Cas had given him some of that warmth. *I nourished him.* "Here." He began to wrap the material around Mirceo's head, forced to smooth a lock of the vampire's hair from his forehead. *I'd rather not know how soft it is.*

After lining up the thin part over Mirceo's heavy-lidded gray eyes, Cas wound the rest of the cloth around Mirceo's neck, nearly smiling when the vampire's Adam's apple bobbed.

Though they'd released some pressure, that chemistry between them had only grown. *What if he's mine?* "There," Cas said in a gruff voice, dropping his hands. He still couldn't believe he was taking young Mirceo into danger. *I've got no choice.* This was the sole way to prevent a kill order on his friend. "You pay attention and you stay alert, okay?" He exhaled with resignation. "Are you ready?"

A smirk in his voice, Mirceo said, "I was born ready, sweetheart."

Cas rolled his eyes.

NINETEEN

The demon traced Mirceo to the mouth of a canyon. The sand-laden winds howled, chasing ribbons of clouds. Moonshadows raced over the shifting dunes.

A few leagues in the distance lay Harea's fortress—a massive pyramid with muted firelight glowing from the few slotted window openings. Smaller structures and a perimeter wall fronted it.

Mirceo gazed at their surroundings in disbelief. His mate had chosen to remain in this wasteland for five centuries. *Rather than be with me.*

Doubt crept in about their future, even after what they'd shared in the cave. What if Caspion viewed that pleasure as Mirceo had once viewed sex?

As just a trade of orgasms.

What if he and the demon *couldn't* make it work? Caspion might have grown too unreasonable over the centuries to be in *any* relationship. Forgodsakes, he'd crushed a priceless talisman to rid himself of Mirceo.

Maybe I'm not . . . enough.

Seeming to sense his unease, Caspion glanced back at him. "What?"

"I thought the cave was bad."

Despite their head wrappings, Mirceo could detect the demon's frown. "Are you having second thoughts about this op?"

"Not about *the op*," he muttered.

"What does that mean?"

"It means that one day you might convince me we have no chance." They stared at each other. *What is he thinking?*

"Noted."

Seriously, demon? "That's all you'll say?"

"If we don't focus for the next couple of hours, someone's going to get killed. Or worse."

"Worse?"

"You want to live out eternity as a Wendigo?" A single bite or scratch from those creatures could transform even an immortal. "Now, look sharp." Caspion began to clap his hands loudly.

"Pardon me, demon, I'm not one to tell you how to do your job—but won't that attract Wendigos?"

More clapping. "Exactly."

"Ah. So we'll be the first in the Lore to voluntarily draw the notice of a legion of these creatures?"

"Yeah."

Mirceo shrugged. "Very well." If the demon said this needed to be done, then so be it. He brandished his sword and fell into place beside Caspion. "Onward!"

Red eyes glowed in the distance as a Wendigo loped out of the canyon toward them. Another followed it. And another. . . .

They had long, stretched-out faces, dripping fangs, and daggerlike claws. Patches of greasy hair grew over their gray skin.

Remnants of clothing clung to their withered, hunchbacked bodies—because they'd once been sentient beings.

As the Wendigos charged, more joined them from behind dunes, their number growing like an avalanche. *Dozens of them.* A wall of the creatures approached from about a hundred feet away.

"Onward?" Caspion demanded, snatching free his sword. "You don't think I'm crazy for drawing *that*?"

Eighty feet away . . .

"There's a fine line between crazy and brave. I trust you in all things—except in relationship matters. Then you must bow down to me."

Fifty feet away . . .

Caspion scanned the wave. "If we live through this, the hunters at the tavern will never believe we took on this many Wendigos. Must be a hundred." He was in attack position, so comfortable with a sword.

Mirceo's gaze would've lingered on the stalwart demon's form, but even he had to take the approaching threat seriously. "They will when I recount our tale. Since I can't lie."

Thirty feet away . . . As the creatures closed in, the blustery winds couldn't dispel their putrid stench.

Caspion slid him a look. "Any immortal with sense would cut and run at this point."

"Leave?" Mirceo scoffed. "You know I'll always fight by your side, demon. In any case, this is the best date I've ever been on."

"We are *not* on a date."

Mirceo laughed.

Ten feet away . . .

Caspion swung for the closest one, beheading it. The creature's brown blood sprayed on the wind. Mirceo got the next one, slicing the Wendigo so fast that its head remained in place until the body toppled over.

Mirceo shared a look with Caspion. *Cool.* "We're tied, old man. But I wager I'll drop more than you."

Voice exhilarated, the demon said, "Oh, you're on, leechling! A fool and his money . . ." He took down one more. And a third. But they kept coming.

Mirceo got busy, tracing into the fray. Soon they were tied at six each. Corpses began to pile up, body parts littering the fight zone.

"Watch where you're stepping! Don't trip over a head."

"Speaking of head"—Mirceo decapitated a hulking Wendigo— "I'll drink from you that way every night for eternity."

As Caspion swung a killing blow, he muttered, "Shouldn't have happened."

"Surely you don't *regret* that pleasure." Mirceo slashed at another Wendigo, dropping it.

The demon felled his as well. "Not many males would regret a blowjob. Doesn't mean I want to repeat it with you."

Lout!

Soon the creatures surrounded them. Mirceo and Caspion drew in, back to back, as they often had when outnumbered in brawls. Mirceo could always predict the demon's sallies and evasive movements, falling into a rhythm with him.

Even as he fought on, Caspion said, "What happened doesn't change anything. I can't *let* it."

"It changes everything! You've come with me four times. Safe to say that you lust for me as much as I do you. Anything else can be managed." *I can learn to be what you need.* Mirceo slew a large male.

Caspion hacked at a particularly belligerent one. "You mean *I* can be managed." Dead Wendigos lay scattered; the living clambered over the massacred to reach them.

"We both can. Aren't relationships made of compromise?" *Slash.*

Slice. "What would a spoiled prince like you know about compromise? When have you ever had to give an inch on anything?"

Swing. "I know I'm ready to for you."

"Above all things"—*jab*—"I want a faithful mate." Caspion dodged razor claws, then struck. "You might think you can be true, but you're too young to know for certain."

Mirceo pivoted, searching for another target. Caspion shifted with him, doing the same. Headless Wendigos twitched all around them—easily more than a hundred—and no more charged them.

Caspion flicked gore from his blade, then sheathed his weapon. From his jacket, he produced a folded tarp. When he spread it over the sand, Mirceo stepped on a corner to keep it from flying off.

With a grunt of thanks, Caspion hauled a Wendigo carcass over it.

"Ah, I see." Mirceo cleaned and sheathed his sword. "You plan to use them as gulg food." Thankful of his gloves, he grabbed the closest body and tossed it beside the other.

As they labored, Caspion said, "You did good back there."

Mirceo couldn't stop his grin. His plan to impress the demon was working!

After collecting a pile of headless corpses, he and Caspion each took a corner of the tarp and started dragging the mass over the sands. The stench was nauseating.

"Listen for a knocking sound," Caspion said as they headed deeper into the valley, ever closer to the fortress. "It's a gulg's jawbone opening."

"Lovely."

"And remember that you can't trace. It's so second-nature you'll try it reflexively."

"I understand. Just for reference, if I need to kill a gulg, where do I strike?"

"You don't. Its brain is supposed to be far below the surface."

Tremors began to vibrate Mirceo's boots. To his right? He snatched a corpse by a wrist and ankle, awaiting a target.

KNOCK KNOCK KNOCK.

A giant fang-filled mouth stretched wide, emitting rancid air. A long, serpentine tongue curled in the gulg's slimy maw. Mirceo tossed the Wendigo, and the jaws snapped shut. The gulg descended once more.

"Good job," Caspion called. They increased their pace. The next gulg was on Caspion's side. He hurled another Wendigo.

SNAP! The mouth slammed closed.

One gulg after another surfaced, each appeased by its meal.

"This is working!" Mirceo tossed another offering. "Where does their territory end?"

"See those red boulders?"

Mirceo squinted against the wind and made out a line of boulders some distance away. He glanced back at the few Wendigos left on the tarp. "We'll run out."

Nod. "Get ready to haul ass. You stay on me like my gods-damned shadow, vampire."

Mirceo grinned behind his scarf. "Eternally, demon."

As soon as Caspion used the last of their bait, he and Mirceo took off. They veered right, then left, dodging yawning mouths and snapping jaws.

Pumping his arms, Mirceo was right behind the demon, following him into *chaos.*

A wind storm had kicked up, gusting sand everywhere. Towering dust devils twisted. All around them: *KNOCK KNOCK KNOCK KNOCK KNOCK KNOCK KNOCK.* The winds distorted the sounds. Dunes crested and toppled over, waves on a sea of tan.

Can't see him!

Caspion yelled, "They're fucking everywhere! Stay with me!"

Mirceo followed the demon's voice. "I'm behind you!" The gulg mouths outnumbered patches of ground. He and Caspion leapt and careened, trying to predict the creatures' movements.

Caspion kept glancing back. "Faster, vampire!"

"Eyes forward, demon!"

"We're almost clear—" *KNOCK KNOCK KNOCK.* Caspion's foot landed atop a gulg just as it opened. He teetered on the lip, arms pinwheeling. Before Mirceo could reach Caspion, a tongue seized the demon's leg and yanked.

Caspion disappeared inside the thing!

Mirceo vaulted to the fang-lined edge. In the large gullet, the demon supported himself with one leg; his other was wedged against the opposite side, holding the creature's jaw open. Caspion had already used his claws to sever the gulg's tongue.

Mirceo didn't think—just dropped down to mirror Caspion's position. The two maneuvered till they were back to back with their legs extended to pry open the jaws. "Now what, demon?"

"Afraid you were going to ask me that."

Mirceo craned his head back. "At least things can't get much worse—"

The gulg started to spin like a saucer.

Caspion bit out, "Still think this is the best date?"

"How will you ever top this?" Blood from Mirceo's stomach rushed to his head as they swirled.

"Lower down, there's a jaw muscle. If we can sever it . . ."

"We walk down like this?"

"That's the plan."

Dizziness reigned, but Mirceo believed in Caspion. In them. Working together, they descended closer to the jaw muscle. But they also neared its throat, which opened and closed below them like a trash compactor.

Mirceo spied a juncture of two bulging tendons. "I can almost reach it." As he pulled free his weapon, the thing spun even faster. With a yell, Mirceo swung his sword, severing the tendons. That side of the gullet sagged.

Tension gone, Mirceo and Caspion dropped from their wedged position. The demon dug his claws into the flesh, holding on with one hand, his other grappling to catch Mirceo.

"I've got a hold!" Mirceo had stabbed his sword for purchase, was now dangling from it. The throat was about to enclose his feet.

Caspion said, "I'm going to toss you out of here! If you can keep the thing open from above, I can leap up."

"Do it." Mirceo clasped forearms with Caspion. Giving the demon his weight, he retrieved his sword with his free hand. They met gazes.

The demon swung him to get momentum . . . right . . . left . . . "GO!"

Mirceo flew upward, tumbling onto the lip. He used his sword to wedge open the taut side. "Come on, demon! Now!"

Caspion dug into the gullet wall with the claws of both hands, bringing up his knees and planting the toes of his boots. His body tensed. Gritting his teeth, he leapt.

He shot up toward Mirceo . . . didn't stop . . . just kept coming . . . He tackled Mirceo and sent them careening onto the sand.

"What the hell, demon?"

They scrambled up. Caspion had taken them past the red boulders! Had any gulgs followed?

The mouths milled about, sucking at the air and colliding into each other. But they'd stopped at that boundary!

"We made it, vampire!" Caspion whaled a slap on his back.

Between breaths, Mirceo said, "Dare I say we're bonding?" *The way to a demon's heart is through the hunt.*

"Here." Caspion had somehow snagged Mirceo's sword on the way out.

"Thanks." He sheathed it once more.

This close to the fortress, the winds had abated somewhat. Caspion tugged off his scarf, so Mirceo did as well.

"Okay, leechling"—the demon's glowing blue eyes crinkled at the sides—"you're on deck."

TWENTY

We actually might survive! Cas and the vampire had a possible shot at *not dying*. Unable to contain his excitement, he clamped Mirceo's shoulder. "You've got this."

He ignored the thoughts that had run through his mind while trapped inside that creature, burying those reflections deep. If he and the prince lived through the rest of the night, Cas would sift through and process them.

For now, he forced his attention to the job. "I think that firelight at the top of the pyramid is the sorcerer's personal chamber. Can you get us inside there?"

"We'll soon find out."

"You see the guardhouse up front?" Cas pointed it out. "The scylla tentacles will emerge just beyond it. The outer wall of the fortress marks the mystical barrier. Let's hope it doesn't affect your mist."

"Otherwise we'll turn corporeal and plummet right into the creature's tentacles?"

"Bingo. The hard part will be getting *in*; we'll likely be able to teleport straight *out* of the fortress."

When Mirceo reached for his hand, Cas hesitated. In conservative Abaddon, he'd never seen two males holding hands.

"Are you jesting?" Mirceo demanded. "Hand holding is taboo—after I nursed blood from your dick?"

Cas had to stifle a groan. *Don't remind me.* He accepted Mirceo's hand, frowning at the way they fit. *If I was born for him, was Mirceo born for me?* "Now what?"

"Now I concentrate," Mirceo answered, tone curt. He drew in a deep breath, then exhaled, closing his eyes. Heartbeats passed.

Damn it, Cas wasn't averse to holding another male's hand, it was just . . . *new.* He recalled the first time he'd sampled lobster. It'd smelled amazing, the tender meat glistening with butter, but he hesitated to try something unfamiliar.

Cas had become set in his ways, but the vampire expected him to accept all these changes without even an afterthought. The temperature began to increase, distracting him. Was the air getting more humid? Mist arose, surrounding them.

A comforting sense of warmth enveloped Cas, as if this bank of vapor blunted all of his concerns. The rest of the world melted into the background—there, but not there. Even the sound of the wind was subdued. Their bodies faded into faint, glittering outlines. "So this is really happening?" *I'm nothing but mist.*

"Fate says you are a Dacian now—so you can join me. We can see, hear, and feel each other, but non-Dacians can't detect us. In theory."

Only the two of them existed inside this cocoon. Cas felt *connected* to the vampire, as he'd never been to anyone else. He wished he could be enfolded like this when he had time to savor it. "I have to admit, this is a damn handy skill." What other jobs could they pull off together?

"Are you ready?"

Cas mimicked Mirceo: "I was born ready, sweetheart." He grinned when the vampire muttered, *"Demonic lout."*

They began to float upward, levitating farther and farther off the ground. Cas had to stifle a laugh. *Amazing!* As they continued to rise like a cloud, they moved toward that boundary.

Closer . . . closer . . . closer . . .

Here—

Tentacles burst from the ground, shooting toward them. *Oh, fuck me!* The scaly snakelike arms coiled around them—through them. *Through our bodies!*

Somehow Cas choked back a yell. He was about to piss himself—how was Mirceo so calm and focused? With steely determination, the prince pressed on.

They outdistanced the scyllas' reach! Cas murmured, "Nice play, vampire. No one has ever gotten this far."

Mirceo didn't react, absorbed by his task.

Still rising, they approached the top of the pyramid. Would he be able to mist them inside? Everything depended on this step—all the work they'd done, all the unwitting prep Cas had completed over the centuries.

They neared . . . then passed through the stone. Cas's senses blanked, a feeling like being momentarily blinded and muffled in cotton. Then . . . flickering light?

Gods almighty, they'd breached Harea's stronghold!

So this is the lair of the notorious King of Sand. A fire illuminated the large chamber. Gold gilded the walls, the hearth encrusted with rubies. A scorpion the size of a small car slept before the fire. Yet more security?

A massive bed levitated a couple of feet above the marble floor. In it, a dozen unclothed females slumbered around the sole male.

The sorcerer.

He was naked as well, passed out beside a large opium pipe. The drug's scent still spiced the air.

The jewel-draped females must be his personal harem. The concubines came in all shapes, sizes, and colors—purple, black, white, blue—like a Miss Lore competition. Was Mirceo's gaze lingering on any of those beauties?

"We're clear," Cas whispered. "I'll take Harea. You get the scorpion. But *pay attention*."

As Mirceo made them solid, gravity weighed them down, their bodies reclaiming mass. The world suddenly seemed harder and colder than before. Mirceo released him, then they both drew their swords.

The scorpion scuttled to life at once. Hissing at their scent, it snapped its claws and hoisted its meaty stinger. Acidic venom dripped from it, searing holes into the floor. Mirceo traced through the acrid smoke to fend off the creature.

As females began to stir on the bed, Cas tucked his sword tip beneath Harea's chin. Yet the sorcerer didn't so much as twitch. Worry for Mirceo distracted Cas.

The scorpion's tail shot forward with blistering speed, but Mirceo was just as quick, blocking the strike with his sword. The vampire wielded his blade as though it were an extension of his body. *Gods, the way he moves. . . .*

Mirceo targeted the scorpion's head; it fended off his sword with its claws, jabbing that tail. The stinger plunged toward Mirceo's leg—

Before Cas could draw a breath, the vampire glided out of the way, and the stinger crashed against the floor inches from one of his boots.

Mirceo took that instant to swing his sword. The tail plopped to the floor, writhing and dribbling acid. He dodged two claw strikes, then planted the tip of his blade into the scorpion's head.

Creature defeated, Mirceo flashed Cas that mind-scrambling grin.

Focus. As more concubines awakened, Cas turned to a blue zalos demoness. "We're here to apprehend Harea. I assume we have the right sorcerer."

"Uh-huh." She showed no distress that Harea was being taken or that their pet scorpion had just been put down. "He probably won't wake. Been on a bender." She canted her head. "How did you get inside? We've watched failed attempts for ages."

"How?" Mirceo answered, striding toward the bed. "We're a soon-to-be-legendary hunting partnership. 'Impossible' is our middle name."

What am I going to do with this vampire? Cas pulled the mystical restraints off his belt, then tossed them to Mirceo. "Bind the prisoner."

Cuffs in hand, the vampire knelt on the bed. "Pardon me, tulips." His grin deepened as he waded on his knees through beautiful females to reach Harea. Instead of fighting to protect their master, the concubines giggled and made eyes at gorgeous Mirceo.

Cas clenched his jaw. *Mind on the job.* Harea was incredibly dangerous.

Or the degenerate *would* be—if he ever woke.

As Mirceo shackled the male's wrists behind his back, Harea mumbled, "Even sorcery . . . can't get my staff hard again. Pipe, females, *PIPE.*" But he didn't rouse.

Mirceo rolled Harea over, his gaze raking over the sorcerer's unclothed body. Harea's olive skin was deeply tanned, and tattooed hieroglyphics marked his chest. He had shoulder-length black hair, wavier than Mirceo's stick-straight locks, and a tall, generously muscled build.

Harea was not a little hung.

Cas scowled at the vampire. "Getting an eyeful?" he said, unable to keep the jealousy out of his tone.

Mirceo winked at him, then asked the harem, "Ladies, will one of you fetch a pair of pants for the sorcerer?"

Another naked concubine—a godsdamned *redheaded nymph*—slid off the bed and sauntered off to retrieve some. As she sashayed back to Mirceo, she held the vampire's eyes.

He gave her a courteous bow. "My thanks, tulip." He began to dress the man, threading Harea's legs into the slim-fitting pants. Cas gritted his teeth when Mirceo had to lean his face down close to the male's groin.

The redhead rejoined the harem on the bed. "If you're taking him away, who will tend to our lusts?"

Mirceo laced the breeches over Harea's member, then grinned at Cas. "It does sound like a quandary, doesn't it, demon?"

"You two should stay for a bit." The redhead's hand dipped between her thighs. "We'll pleasure you so hard that you'll never want to leave us." The others murmured encouragement.

"Will you, indeed?" Mirceo said with a devilish light in his eyes. "Tell us more, tulip. . . ."

TWENTY-ONE

"Tulip? *Tulip?*" the demon snapped at Mirceo. "Why do you call females that?" In the alley behind the Red Flag, Caspion dropped the still-unconscious sorcerer onto the grimy bricks. Harea hadn't so much as twitched when they'd teleported him from Poly.

The weather between dimensions had gone from freezing grit to muggy fog. In this plane, mere seconds had passed since Mirceo and Caspion had left.

Mirceo leaned against a lamppost, grinning at the demon's jealousy. "Because they love it when I do."

As they awaited the Gaolers, Caspion kept his sword at the ready. "Are you going to continue fucking them? They also *love* it when you do that."

"I only have eyes for you." Sometime over the last three nights, Mirceo's fascination with his mate had escalated into . . . hero worship. Whenever he gazed at the demon, he was almost *humbled* that fate had connected them.

Caspion paced the alley. "Perhaps at present."

Who could compete with such a warrior? One day Mirceo would convince the stubborn demon that he would be faithful. "There's a difference between trifling and fucking, love. A bevy of beauties was flirting with me, and I flirted back—a touch. Face it, my charm's the only thing that got us out of there with our virtue intact."

Caspion shook his head hard. "You're a player. You always will be."

"This jealousy of yours is *delicious*." Mirceo licked his bottom lip.

The demon's gaze locked it. "You're never going to change."

"Exchanging repartee is a far cry from plowing through them all."

Caspion slowed his pacing. "Did you . . . did you want to?"

"No. Not whatsoever." They both knew he couldn't lie.

"And Harea? You couldn't have gotten your mouth closer to the sorcerer's dick without biting it." Caspion's fierce expression made Mirceo's toes curl in his boots.

"One more time: I want my mate alone."

"Why would you clothe Harea?"

"Seemed like a decent thing to do. Hell, demon, a few months ago, we might have befriended a hedonist like him. And for the record—I was *trying* to make you jealous."

"Maybe I'm not jealous. Maybe I'm pissed because you keep throwing out this idea that we're fated—yet your behavior doesn't back that up whatsoever. I'm too old for bullshit."

"Your pique isn't surprising. Your demonic temper will continue to get more volatile the longer you go without claiming your mate." He pointed a thumb at himself. "Claiming *me*."

"*If* you are mine."

"Uh-huh." The demon wasn't going down without a fight. But that was okay. Mirceo had always savored a good conquest. He'd first viewed Caspion as *only* a conquest. One day Mirceo would have to come clean about that wager. *And about the demon's last night in Dacia.*

But for now . . . "What about you? Did you desire the concubines?"

He so clearly wanted to lie. But other than when he denied his feelings, Caspion had always been honest with Mirceo. "Why wouldn't I? I'm not mated."

Deflection! "It's a simple question. Did you want any—or all—of them?"

"My mind was on the job." Caspion's scowl deepened as Mirceo's grin spread.

"Right. Back to the job. Should we have a plan in place for when the Gaolers show?"

"Yeah, the plan is: let Caspion do the talking."

Mirceo gave a mock bow. The demon could be overly domineering—nature of the beast—but luckily Mirceo had a more laid-back disposition. *Such a change from how I used to be when young.*

Otherwise he and Caspion would never make it. Now more than ever, Mirceo believed they would. Yes, seeing the hell his mate had called home had undermined his confidence. But the two of them had triumphed over incredible odds. Mirceo had pulled his weight and demonstrated that he could be an asset—

Harea heaved. Vomit spewed from his lips onto the street. And still he didn't wake. Brows drawn, the sorcerer mumbled, "Dragon's breath. Apocalypse. Nightside is real."

Mirceo chuckled. "I think we did that harem a favor. . . ." He trailed off when his breaths condensed into puffs of smoke. In this warm air? "Caspion?"

The demon's alert gaze swept over their surroundings. "I see it."

Mirceo stepped back to view the larger side street beyond this alleyway, his eyes going wide. A garbageman was poised with a can over his head, motionless, the truck's compactor suddenly silent. "Time's standing still." The driver had been pouring coffee out of his window—the fluid hung suspended in midair—when he'd been frozen in place.

Caspion gave a curt nod, reaching for Mirceo. "Closer to me, vampire."

Not a problem. He'd just traced to the demon's side when four males appeared. Wearing frayed black cloaks, the phantasms sat astride ghostly horses.

The Gaolers.

Hello, fodder of all future nightmares. They looked like skeletal reapers—at first glance. But then Mirceo realized their ragged faces had been tattooed to look like skulls. In places, inked flesh had peeled from actual bone. Both they and their mounts appeared to be decomposing. They had no eyeballs, but seemed to possess sight.

Caspion sidled in front of Mirceo protectively—*awww*—and boldly announced, "We claim the bounty on this sorcerer, the King of Sand."

At last Harea began to come to with a pained groan. Twisting on the ground, he slurred, "Where'm I?"

May I never get that high. At least, not without Caspion to watch his back.

Harea tried to rise, finally managing to sit upright. "The hell's going on?" Swinging his head toward Mirceo and Caspion, he said, "Who're you?" His bleary eyes were a golden color, shot through with red.

Mirceo felt for the male. To go to sleep buried in trim, then wake to a capture and decomposing jailers? Harsh. "I'm Mirceo Daciano. My *mate* and I have captured you for the bounty. No hard feelings."

"Can't be." Harea's head snapped toward the Gaolers. "No." Visible chill bumps arose over the sorcerer's dark skin. He grappled against the restraints. Light glowed in his palms, but the shackles deactivated his powers. Sobering swiftly, he faced Mirceo and Caspion again. "I'll kill you two for this! I'll destroy anything you care about and murder anyone you love." Lips drawn back from his teeth, he hissed, "I'll replace the blood in your veins with sand!"

"Note to self"—Mirceo tapped his temple—"beware of the sand man."

One of the Gaolers raised a putrefying hand. A drawstring coin bag materialized above his palm. Without a word, he dropped the clinking bag at Caspion's feet.

Harea met Mirceo's eyes a last time. He mouthed, *You're a dead man.*

The Gaolers—and the sorcerer—disappeared.

Out in the side street, the garbage truck's compactor roared to life. Releasing a pent-up breath, Caspion sheathed his sword, then dipped to collect the coin bag. He hefted the weight, smiling at the metallic jingle.

"That's what I'd call a no-nonsense transaction." The tension in Mirceo's knotted muscles faded. "We make a good team, demon."

Caspion hiked his shoulders. "We completed a tough job."

"Tough? You called it impossible, one of the longest-standing bounties in the Lore. You said no one could get close to that sorcerer. And so on and so forth."

Caspion opened the bag and investigated the contents. "I'll be damned. It's real dragon gold."

"I've never seen it before." Mirceo traced closer for a look. "It truly is red." The coins had been struck with the image of flames. "If neither of us needs the money, you should give these to your friend Bettina. Wouldn't a goldsmith like her enjoy it?"

"She would go insane for this." All Sorceri worshipped gold, but Bettina doubly so. "You'd really give up your share for her?"

"Of course."

"I'm surprised you remember what I told you about her passion. You always seemed to be in your own little world whenever I opened up."

"Because I was committing every word to memory."

Surprise flashed in the demon's expression. "You . . . can't lie."

"I told you I was interested in your mind. Your divine body and blood are simply the cherries on top."

For long moments, Caspion stared at Mirceo. Seeming to make a decision, the demon said, "I think it's time to celebrate."

TWENTY-TWO

DRINK!"

At a crowded table inside the Red Flag, Cas and the vampire raised their cups, then emptied them.

Earlier, when Cas had pinned the bounty parchment on the board for completed jobs, all the hunters had clamored to buy him and Mirceo rounds.

For a few hours Cas had been able to forget his history with the prince and enjoy his company. He didn't know what tomorrow would bring, but tonight he'd been proud of Mirceo—as only a friend would be.

Lie to yourself, Cas.

To the very fucking end.

"Come on, vampire," said one of the demon hunters. "Divvy how you stole into the sorcerer's lair."

These pros had been stunned to hear that Cas and Mirceo had taken out more than a hundred Wendigos. And that'd only been the first step.

Mirceo cast them his arrogant, sexy-as-hell grin. "Trade secret." His words were slurred—because the vampire was drinking *demon brew.*

That libation provided an even buzz, right up until the bomb of total drunkenness hit. Cas had begun monitoring his own consumption. In the past, one of them had always remained a touch more sober in case they ran into threats.

Earlier, Cas had taken him outside, telling him, "You don't have to drink every time they toast us. And you sure as hell don't have to down brew. It gains on you with every drop."

Mirceo had grazed his finger over Cas's collarbone, saying, "My aim is to impress your friends."

He already had. "Color them impressed. Besides, Bettina is the only friend I care about, apart from you."

"Are we friends?"

"We could be, if you were content to remain that way."

"Hmm." What did that mean? "Even after what happened in the cave?"

He'd had no answer for that.

"Admit it, demon. You're having fun with me. Just as we always used to."

"I don't deny that." The vampire made life more exciting. Made each second taste better. If he was honest, Cas would admit this might be the best day of his life.

Unequaled bounty. Unequaled pleasure.

Unequaled mate? No! There was still hope for self-preservation. . . .

"Can I tell them you're mine?" Mirceo had asked.

"Sure you don't want to keep your options open, *tulip*?"

Mirceo had grabbed Cas's balls.

GULP. "Easy, vampire."

Mirceo had given them a tug that sent Cas rocking to his toes. "I'd like to tell the world that these are mine. That all of you belongs to me."

The vampire's show of possessiveness had been . . . *thrilling*.

Now a lion shifter leaned in toward Mirceo and said, "At least tell us how you got past the sand scyllas." That shifter was irritatingly bewitched with the sophisticated prince.

In fact, all of the rough-and-tumble hunters were, which made Cas's own possessiveness—already off the charts—spike even higher.

Mirceo had pointed out that Cas's demonic temper would continue to grow more volatile. *Too true.*

"It was nothing." Mirceo brushed imaginary lint off his shoulder. "A day in the life of bounty hunters such as we."

Cas's lips twitched. Throughout the night, the vampire's lids had grown heavy, his grin permanent and crooked. He was kind of . . . adorable like this.

"Were you truly inside a gulg?" another hunter asked.

"Come, gentlemen, who among us *hasn't* been?" Mirceo winked at Cas.

The charmed hunters laughed. They reminded him of the fawning group that had surrounded the prince the first night Cas had met him.

"Now, which one of you exterminated that giant scorpion?" Leyak asked as he poured another round.

Cas waved toward the vampire. "The scorpion was all him."

With his eyes lively, Mirceo said, "I also faced a monster in a firelit cave, a notorious one-eyed beast. I thought for sure it'd take me; it had me on my knees till I bested it with my fangs."

Cas coughed into his fist to disguise his laugh.

Before anyone could ask about this *beast*, Mirceo said to them, "Tell me more about my hunting partner's exploits."

"He took his first posted bounty"—Leyak waved at the wall of them—"when he was just fourteen. But his big break was finding a rich warlock's daughter."

Mirceo said, "This I must hear." Did Cas like that the vampire hung on every word as others talked about him?

Hell. Yes. Sometimes Mirceo gazed at Cas as if he was a hero of old—as if the vampire was a little . . . awed by him.

Feels like I've waited my entire godsdamned life for a look like that.

"She'd last been seen in a dark forest," Leyak said. "In his panic, the warlord sent out his whole settlement to search for her."

One of the hunters muttered, "Polluting the trail. Rookie mistake."

"Even so, Cas located her," Leyak continued. "She'd tripped into an abandoned troll hole and gotten trapped."

"How did you find her?" Mirceo asked.

Deadpan, Cas said, "Tripped into the same troll hole."

The hunters laughed, Mirceo among them.

Gods, that vampire's laugh turned Cas *inside out.*

Leyak shook his head. "Nothing doing. Caspion identified her footprints among thousands of them and tracked her alone."

Easy enough. Her right leg had been longer than her left, and her shoes had been assembled instead of cobbled—a sign of great wealth in that dimension.

"Tell me more," Mirceo said.

"There's a reason he's called Caspion *the* Tracker," Leyak said with pride. "He's collected on every bounty, locating his every prey."

Over the rim of his cup, Cas said, "Except for the one that got away."

Leyak sighed. "Not technically a bounty, son."

"Who got away?" Mirceo asked.

"The Vrekeners who attacked Bettina," Cas said bitterly. "Remember, I could never find them—"

"Because you can't bloody fly," Leyak said, and the others nodded. "Their realm floated in the skies."

"Maybe even then I could have succeeded." Narrowing his eyes at Mirceo, he said, "But someone beat me to the punch."

The vampire muttered, "Trehan."

Bingo. That prick had brought Bettina the heads of her attackers. He must've located the gang with his scry crystal, then utilized his skill as an assassin to slaughter them.

Before his good mood soured further, Cas stood. "Enough out of you lot. I need to get my friend home." They booed Cas, but he wouldn't be deterred. Taking Mirceo's arm, he said, "Time to call it, leechling. You've drunk your fill."

Gray eyes locked on Cas's neck, Mirceo rasped, "Never."

TWENTY-THREE

W here are we?" The vampire peered around Cas's beach bungalow.

"Another one of my bolt holes." A far cry from the luxury Mirceo was used to, this no-frills cabin had only one bedroom, a kitchen, and a bathroom. But the deck was large, stretching out over the sea.

"You brought me to another hideout?" Mirceo slurred. "We must be getting serious, then."

"Don't read anything into it. It isn't like I can trace you home. Come on, I'm putting you to bed."

"Which side do you sleep on, sweetheart? I'm flexible. If there's not enough room, I invite you to sleep *atop* me."

Mercy. "Even if we weren't to remain solely friends, I wouldn't take advantage of you when you're in this condition."

Mirceo cast him that crooked grin. "If I say pretty please?"

"You'd hate me in the morning."

Growing serious, he said, "I could never hate you."

Nor I you. Though Cas had wanted to. How much easier that would be. Even when he'd believed Mirceo had betrayed him, he'd still missed the vampire. "I told you that brew gains on you with every drop. It's about to hit. You'll soon be comatose."

Mirceo squinted. "Are those holes in the walls?"

"Maybe a couple." Cas's earlier frustration seemed a lifetime ago. He could never have predicted what had been in store for him.

The vampire's sweet, piercing bite . . .

Keep control, Cas. He helped Mirceo out of his coat, then sat him down on the bed. "Arms above your head." Mirceo dutifully complied, and Cas pulled his shirt off.

"I like it when you take care of me, demon."

"You need someone to look out for you," Cas said, then bit his tongue. *I'm not going to be that male.* He quickly added, "Because you often act like an unthinking child."

"Fair point." Mirceo leaned down and attempted to remove a boot, failed, then tried again.

Chuckling, Cas knelt to help him.

"Thanks. They seem damnably complex right now."

Cas pulled them off. "Uh-huh." He grabbed Mirceo's ankles and tossed the vampire's legs up onto the bed.

Mirceo sank back. "The pillow smells like Caspion." He buried his face against it, inhaling deeply. When he looked at Cas again, his eyes flickered with desire. "My dreams will be filthy." He couldn't look more tempting. Reading his mind, Mirceo said, "You like the way I look in your bed."

Where you belong. Inner shake. "Arrogant leech." He pulled the covers up to Mirceo's chin.

The vampire shoved them down to his waist. "Not a denial. Now that you know I'm yours, it's not safe to ignore your instincts much longer."

There was still hope. . . .

"We must fuck just to preserve your sanity." He sighed. "The things I do for my 'friends.'"

"Enough of that."

Mirceo started shucking his pants. "Can't sleep confined."

Mercy! To distract himself, Cas snagged a blanket to cover the french doors against the coming light of dawn. They faced west, but he'd take no chances. Another blanket for the side window. Once he'd sun-proofed the room, he turned back.

Mirceo's pants were on the floor, and he had the covers up to his waist again.

Thank gods. "You need to sleep."

Relaxation had stolen over the vampire's body, but he wasn't ready to pass out yet. "Stay with me."

"Should I read you a bedtime story too, leechling?"

"Do you have erotic ones in your repertoire? Perhaps an original."

"You have an answer for everything."

Mirceo waved at the blankets. "You really do care about me, don't you?"

Cas pulled a chair up to the bed. "Because I don't want my drunken vampire friend to fry under my watch?" He removed his own boots, then kicked back. He would sleep out on the deck tonight. Not in the bed with Mirceo. *NOT in the bed.*

"Aside from my parents and Mina, you're the only person *I* have ever cared deeply about. After my mother and father were murdered, I fairly much hated everyone. Growing up in Dacia didn't help matters."

"Do you know who killed them?" Mirceo had said only that a cowardly royal had taken their lives.

"My uncle Stelian's father beheaded them in their sleep."

Was Cas better off not knowing his parents than to have lost them so brutally? "Why?"

"Millennia ago, a princess in our family cursed the Dacianos to infight and destroy ourselves until we crowned the rightful heir—Lothaire. For generations, Dacianos schemed and manipulated to seize the throne, and I'm sure my parents weren't innocent." Frowning to himself, he said, "I think Trehan hunted down Stelian's murderous father to protect Mina and myself."

"That all sounds insane."

"Imagine raising a little girl under that threat. It's why I'm so protective of Mina. We've had targets on our backs since we were born. And then, with our parents out of the way, I feared our uncles would circle us like sharks."

"You were just fifteen." At least no one had wanted to *kill* Cas when he'd been that age. "What did you do?"

"Turned into an angry stick-in-the-mud. I toed every line and never lowered my guard. I didn't fuck for the first time until I was twenty."

Cas couldn't wrap his mind around this. "So you've only had ten years of partners." His mood plummeted. A rake like Mirceo likely wouldn't settle down for an eternity. A rake who hadn't gotten the lead out *never* would. "And then what happened?"

A soft, fond smile curled Mirceo's lips. "Mina won them over, one by one. Viktor, the head of the army, caught her—a little imp—devising brilliant battle strategies with her dollies. He lost his heart. From the time she was eight, she carried a blade, so Trehan, the shadow assassin, lost his as well." Mirceo couldn't sound prouder. "She brought blood mead to the guardhouse for Stelian, the realm's gatekeeper—because she felt sorry for him. She admitted that she would keep watch with that lonely oaf, just sitting in silence and observing the mist float by. It eventually became clear that they'd all die for her."

Cas could see this. Timid, blushing Mina kindled a person's protective instincts.

"Once I realized my sister was in no danger from them, I loosened up, becoming the hedonist you once knew."

"You bring out such protectiveness as well."

"Do I? Mina and I are two of a kind," he said. "Dacians consider Trehan the kingdom's sword, Viktor its wrath, Stelian its sentinel, and Lothaire its cunning. Our people see Mina and me as the beating heart of Dacia. That's why most are helpless not to love us."

Beginning to believe that. "Your partners always fell for you."

"Hmm."

"Hmmm, what?"

"The day I told Mina that our parents were gone, I comprehended that I was all she had in the world. I promised her that *I* would be her mother and father. She gazed up at me with . . . *unlimited expectation* and said, 'I believe you.'"

My gods, Cas could barely imagine the pressure. Mirceo had been so young.

Mirceo frowned. "Partners often cast me a similar look of expectation after sex, as if they'd pinned all their worldly hopes on me. The burden of that responsibility filled me with panic and resentment—but I never understood why. Now I do."

"What do you understand?"

Their gazes held. "They wanted me to give them something that already belonged to another. They wanted my future—but it's yours alone."

Cas loosed a breath. "So if *I* were ever to look at you like that . . ."

"Demon, you can pin any worldly hopes on me"—his voice grew hoarse—"because I've already pinned mine on you."

What if the vampire truly would treat a mate differently? Wasn't that the way of matehood?

Mirceo's lids slid shut, the brew about to drop the hammer. "Caspion, I was proud of you tonight. Proud that you're mine."

The prince continued to see him as strong and capable, having no idea what a wretched creature his mate had once been. Mirceo's description of royal intrigues just reminded Cas how ignoble his blood was.

He's the heir to an ancient line from an extraordinary realm; I don't even have a family name.

Mirceo murmured, "Before I pass out, I give you full permission to take advantage of me. You know I'm not shy. Look your fill. Touch. Do whatever you want to me."

Here for my use. All night Cas had been half erect; now he grew painfully hard.

"And I'm always ready to blood-take if you need my services."

His words brought on a mixture of irritation and lust. Again the vampire was eroding Cas's control. "I'll keep that in mind." He yanked the covers up to Mirceo's chin once more.

"Maybe I'll sleep for just a moment. . . ." Any remaining tension drained from his body.

Down for the count. *So leave him. Go to another property. Get away.*

Cas stood to pace. The last thing he needed was to get in even deeper with this male. *At least leave the fucking room.*

Instead he returned to the chair, pulling it even closer.

Mirceo's lips were parted, his lashes thick against his cheeks. He was always smirking or laughing, his expressions changeable. At rest, he seemed even younger than his thirty years.

From the very beginning, Cas had found Mirceo Daciano's face spellbinding, but right now there was a sweetness to it that called to him.

He didn't know how long he'd stared, but gradually the vampire began to grow restless. He changed positions, then again, and moisture dotted his forehead. *Sweating out the brew.*

Cas traced to the bathroom and wet a cloth. He returned to sit on the edge of the bed, then smoothed the cloth over Mirceo's brow.

Though Cas's body still thrummed with desire, caring for the sleeping prince soothed his mind. He brushed the backs of his knuckles Mirceo's cheek, testing this affection.

More than instinct was at work here. When he imagined Mirceo as a scared teenage boy in Dacia, tenderness and protectiveness surged inside Cas. Those feelings reminded him of his frenzied thoughts when they'd been trapped in that gulg: *I'll make this monster choke on my fucking bones before I let it have the vampire. I'll die for Mirceo.*

A gust of breath left his lungs. No longer could Cas deny what he knew was true. He was a vampire's mate, and Mirceo was . . . a demon's.

Mine. Acceptance. *This male is mine.*

Without attempting him, Cas couldn't confirm their connection a hundred percent, but he *felt* their bond. He'd never been so sure about anything.

This sleeping prince is my fated one.

For so long Cas had wondered what his mate would look like. Why not explore Mirceo? The vampire had all but dared him to.

Drawing down the sheet, Cas bared his torso. Running the cloth lower, he let his gaze roam over Mirceo's lean body.

The elegant column of his throat. The broad chest with not an ounce of spare flesh. Those flat, dusky nipples.

All of this pale, sleek perfection is mine.

He gave himself permission to study Mirceo's body—with intent. He'd never assessed another male with the thought of enjoying him—of fighting or killing him, yes, but never considering the things he fantasized about with Mirceo.

He imagined kissing the vampire's neck, nipping it with his fangs. His lips would travel down Mirceo's chest, following in the wake of the cloth. He'd suck those dusky nipples raw. He'd dip his tongue to that shallow navel. Nuzzle the trail of black hair beneath it.

Cas would play with the prince, teasing him, dominating him. At the thought, his cock pulsed in his pants.

He audibly swallowed as he inched the sheet down to reveal Mirceo's member. The veined shaft was semihard, the taut crown a shade of plum. The vampire's size was generous, nearly as long as Cas's but slimmer. Back in their days of debauchery, more than one immortal had screamed while riding it.

Again, Cas looked at it with . . . intent. What would that flesh taste like? What would it be like to suckle that length? Cas grazed his fingertips over his lips as he envisioned pleasuring another male with his mouth.

He would pin Mirceo's hips down, then tease and tongue him for hours. After much suffering, Mirceo would be allowed to come.

Cas recalled the addictive taste of Mirceo's seed and knew he'd drink the vampire down.

The idea made his shaft *throb*.

Just as Cas reached for his mate's cock, Mirceo turned to his front, revealing the planes of his back. *And lower.* Cas groaned.

He'd never been the type to obsess over a woman's ass. Yet Mirceo's flawless ass held him rapt.

The small of the vampire's back rose to curves of sculpted muscles with shadowed hollows on the sides. The flesh at the cleft was so taut that Cas wondered if he could even graze a fang there.

He'd enjoyed anal sex with females, but he'd never been with a virgin—in any sense of the word. Mirceo would be so unbelievably tight. Cas would need to go slow. Lubrication would be key.

Fantasies arose. Inching his oiled shaft into Mirceo's virgin channel . . . feeding his length in to the hilt . . . fucking moans out of the prince . . . marking the vampire's neck . . . ejaculating inside his mate for the first time . . .

An involuntary growl burst from Cas's chest. In a lather to mount Mirceo, he clenched his fists.

Realization struck: he desired Mirceo more than he did females. More than all others put together. The last time he'd yearned for something this much, he'd literally been starving. Cas was starving *for Mirceo*. He did not make that comparison lightly.

How much longer could Cas resist the irresistible? His gaze flicked to the pale column of Mirceo's neck. For all of the vampire's perfection, he lacked one thing.

My mark.

What if Cas seized what was right before him? His mate. Their future. *I could claim and mark him as soon as he wakes.*

But if the vampire later strayed . . . There was supposed to be no greater pain than a fated one's betrayal.

A mate's *death*? That pain would be short-lived because a demon would follow.

Yet a rift in the bond between mates delivered anguish without equal.

His arousal flagged. *The prince will leave me broken.*

Before Cas did anything stupid, maybe he should explain to Mirceo the harsh realities of matehood.

The totality of it. The eternity of it. The *monogamy* of it.

He'd have that vampire running in the opposite direction.

TWENTY-FOUR

Mirceo dreamed. Even in sleep, he knew he was experiencing his mate's past.

A memory arose from a time years ago when the demon had been just a pup—a time before he'd been known as Caspion. . . .

Standing on his toes, Beggar stared through the tavern window as a barmaid brought steaming food to a nearby table.

Why was he doing this to himself? Seeing what he could never have just made his hunger worse. Look away.

From a tray, the female set out platter after platter. Haunches of venison. Fat sausages. Juicy suckling pig and roasted boar.

He'd just lost a baby fang, but his other one sharpened as he imagined what that meat would taste like. When the scents reached him, his mouth watered. So did his eyes.

If I could have just a shred of that meat . . .

Those demons—a group of five males—were so lucky. They chose when to eat and where. They read symbols on a menu, then picked whatever they were in the mood for. They decided if they would like the table beside the hearth fire.

Beggar wanted to choose. Anything.

He didn't pick which clothes he wanted to wear; he had only the rags on his back. He didn't choose among which shoes he'd wear; he had none at all. The snow and ice bit into his bare feet.

Everyone called him Beggar, because that's how he'd survived. But only in the past. Now he'd learned how to scavenge too.

Cheeks heating, he admitted to himself he'd soon go back to shameful begging if the weather got any colder. One day, when he never had to wear rags or beg anymore, he would give himself a new name, a proud name—

A customer inside met gazes with him, a demon with gouged horns.

Now I'm in trouble! *Last week, the tavern owner had chased him off with a broom! Beggar darted toward the back-alley crate he considered home.*

"Hold there, pup," a male called in a nice-enough tone.

Beggar slowed and turned warily.

The demon with the gouged horns was crossing the icy street toward him. "Come here, son." Gouge carried a piled-high platter!

Sidling closer, Beggar stayed ready to bolt.

"You surely are a filthy little thing. Are you hungry?"

"Yes, sir." His stomach growled loudly, but he was too dazed to be embarrassed. Just a shred of meat . . . He could almost taste it. *Beggar was so focused on the platter that he barely noticed Gouge's four friends emerging from the tavern as well.*

"Do you want this meal, boy?" Gouge asked. "I'll let you have it."

"Y-you will???" This would be riches beyond his imaginings! He was ashamed when tears of gratitude welled in his eyes.

"In exchange for something."

Beggar drew back. He'd learned to hate the wealthy. They amused themselves with people like him, playing games with the poor just because they could. "For what?"

Gouge shared a smirk with his friends, then faced him again. "Follow us, and I'll tell you."

Chills raced over Beggar, but the scent of that food made him trail after the demons. Why were they heading toward the necessary? Nothing good could come from this.

So why am I still following?

Inside the stinking latrine, Gouge said, "If you want this feast, Beggar, you have to eat it with a little spice." He held up the platter.

Tears spilled down Beggar's face, because he knew what would come next. No, no, no—

Gouge turned the platter over, precious food dropping into the latrine.

Steam from piss rose along with the steam from food.

"I wouldn't tarry a moment, whelp," Gouge said, to his friends' laughter. "Each moment fouls your feast even more."

Sobbing, Beggar went to his hands and knees. Vowing that he would never know this humiliation again . . . he ate.

Mirceo shot upright, fangs and claws as sharp as razors. He darted his eyes, surprised not to be in that reeking latrine.

He would find those fucks, and he would godsdamned slaughter them!

Where was Caspion now? He surveyed the room, then scented the air for him. *Not here.*

But he'd return soon. Surely.

Grappling to rein in his emotions, Mirceo scrubbed his forearm over his eyes, recalling every detail of what he'd just experienced.

Caspion had been such a tiny pup, his emaciated body and

rags no match for the cold. Mirceo now knew what it felt like to be chilled to the bone and wracked with ceaseless hunger. He now understood *torment*.

And then those demons had exploited that pain, adding more. Those *dead* demons. *I will stalk them as mist and sever their fucking heads.*

Was it any wonder that Caspion longed for the respect of the Abaddonae? Or that the demon was dominant? He'd lacked power for so long that he now needed to wield it over a partner.

With that dream, Mirceo had taken his mate's past inside him. In a way, he'd made that past his own. Nothing could ever break that bond. Yet for now, he would keep his new knowledge to himself. If Caspion learned Mirceo had seen his memory, he would grow furious.

Mirceo would add this secret to his others: *You were once the subject of a wager, Caspion. And to get you in bed, I resorted to underhanded means. . . .*

Where in the hells was the demon?

As Mirceo rose and yanked on his pants, he tried to piece together the fuzzy parts from last night. Hadn't Caspion explored his body? Or had that been a sweet reverie? Maybe Mirceo had only dreamed the demon's care.

No, the blankets still covered the windows. He traced to one, peeking past the material, wincing at the glare. Full day outside.

Where exactly am I? He spied a shell beach and sun-dappled, turquoise water. Movement at the shoreline caught his eye. *Caspion.*

He was rising from the waves, looking fresh from a swim. *And I can't join him.* Though the light burned his gaze, Mirceo still stared.

He wished that Caspion as a pup could somehow have known he would grow into this proud, magnificent warrior.

Caspion waded shoreward past the breakers, water sluicing over his glorious naked body and bronzed skin. His flat, rose-colored nipples were hardened. From the chill water? The sea's temperature had no effect on Caspion's member. That semihard shaft swayed with each of his steps. The curls at the base gleamed gold in the light.

As Mirceo's gaze lovingly took in every inch of that breathtaking body, he muttered to himself. "My mate's a fucking god."

I want him close always. I want to avenge his childhood pain. I want him in our bed, gazing down at me with those piercing eyes. I want his yells of pleasure ringing in my ears, and his blood heating my veins. . . .

But something was troubling the demon. Caspion's shoulders were knotted, his lips a thin line. He disappeared from the beach; seconds later the shower in the bungalow bathroom began to run.

Mirceo contemplated joining him, but something about Caspion's demeanor held him back. He turned from the window, his gaze flicking over the bag of coins on the bedstand—their bounty. Had Mirceo said or done something amiss during their night of celebration?

No. He rarely made mistakes. And whenever he did, others were eager to forgive him.

A short while later, the shower stopped. Caspion strode into the bedroom with a towel around his waist. He barely glanced at Mirceo.

"Demon, I . . ." *I'm falling for you. I need to protect you always—*

Caspion pushed past him without a word, then snagged a pair of jeans from a closet.

"What's going on, sweetheart?"

That towel dropped, revealing the sun-kissed curves of the demon's chiseled ass. Mirceo had to shuffle his feet to keep from falling over. *Want to bite those mouthwatering cheeks . . .*

Too soon, Caspion drew his pants up, buttoning the fly. He pulled on a black T-shirt, then faced Mirceo. "We need to talk." His demeanor remained icy.

"What's happened?"

"We are going to sort some things out." He strode from the bedroom into the kitchen. Sitting down at the rough-hewn table, he waved to the other chair.

Mirceo sat. "Caspion, you can't keep denying what you know is true. You know we're mates." Now the demon would rail that Mirceo wasn't his, and the two of them would quarrel—

"I want you to leave."

"Pardon?" Mirceo went cold. Damn it, they'd made strides yesterday! "What happened between the time I went to sleep and now?" Comprehension dawned. "You've *accepted* that I'm your mate, haven't you?" The dynamics between them *had* shifted last night!

Caspion steepled his fingers, a contemplative gesture, but his dark claws had grown razor-sharp. His blue eyes flickered to obsidian and back. The demon was in turmoil, only feigning control. "I have." *At last!* "Yet you will still leave. You're going to take a century to do whatever you need to do. Don't toe the line, don't live within boundaries. Fuck anyone who tempts you and continue reveling with your hedonistic . . . friends. At the end of one hundred years, you and I will meet outside the castle in Abaddon. At that time, you will commit to me."

Mirceo's lips parted. "A century apart? Are you insane?"

"This is the only logical route."

"Logical? *Vampires* are supposed to be logical, not claim-deprived *demons*."

"I refuse to share my mate."

Even in the midst of all the craziness Caspion was spouting,

Mirceo loved how "my mate" sounded coming from the demon. "As do I. We will both be faithful."

· Caspion shook his head. "You're not capable of that. At least, not yet. You're too young, too rash, and too selfish. You and I met each other too soon."

"If you know I'm your mate, then you know you can't go that long without fulfilling your instinct to claim me. You'll grow crazed."

Caspion traced to his feet to pace, a muscle ticking in his jaw. "Let me worry about that."

Mirceo stood as well. "I'm not agreeing to this. Forget it."

Lips drawn back from his fangs, Caspion said, "Once I claim you, I will never let you go. I will mark you—for all time."

Mirceo had never seen him this livid. "That's what I want!"

Caspion lunged for him, pressing him up against the wall. "For once, *THINK*!" he roared. "This isn't a bloody game. If we don't part, I will claim you. Once you wear my mark, you will never fuck another. Never bite another. Your life will never be the same!"

"You lout, I *want* my life to never be the same! We will build a new life together." *Adding to the House of Castellan. Pups. A family.* Mirceo dared to lay his palm over the demon's thundering heart.

Caspion flinched as though burned, but allowed the contact. Gods, the emotions crossing those stormy eyes . . . need, hope, despair. "I see the future clearly, vampire, because I know you so well. Once I claim you, your panic will return, and you will leave. Then I'll be just like all of your other conquests, the ones who would give anything for just one more night with you."

"None of them was my mate! And you're my best friend on top of that. Why can't you believe in me?"

"Because you've taught me not to." Caspion released him and

backed away. "Do you know what tracking is at its most basic form? It's the ability to recognize potential when you come across it. I see so much potential in you, vampire. But you are not there yet. For now, you are your own worst enemy."

"What will it take to change your mind?"

"Nothing. Your next step is to leave. A hundred years can pass quickly for an immortal who remains active."

Bullshit. "I'm going to take a *short* leave just to get you off my back about it. I will carefully consider every aspect of our future. And then I will return in four days."

Caspion shook his head hard. "One hundred years—"

"Four. Days." Mirceo pinned his gaze. "Face it, demon, neither of us will make it a week apart, much less a century."

TWENTY-FIVE

The first two days of their separation had been *excruciating.*

A low roar constantly sounded in Cas's ears. Part of him thought/hoped that Mirceo would consider everything, realize he couldn't yet commit, and stay away.

But another hot, aching part of Cas prayed to every dark god that the vampire would return in another two days.

Put me out of this misery. Cas hadn't been able to eat or sleep. He'd finally started bloodletting—slice marks in various stages of regeneration covered his forearms—but the relief was fleeting. As he'd stared at the crimson pouring down the sink drain, he'd regretted the waste, just as he would the waste of any nourishment. It reminded him of Gouge, a demon who'd offered food, only to throw it away.

Cas could concentrate on nothing, his instincts going haywire. *Need a distraction.* His gaze landed on the coin pouch. Cas would go see Bettina, dropping off the dragon gold.

Stuffing the pouch into his coat pocket, he traced into her

light and airy workshop. Her specialty was body jewelry with hidden weaponry. Dress dummies had been arrayed with various pieces. Workbenches with intricate tools lined the walls.

Wearing protective goggles, Bettina sat hunched over one of her creations, engraving the piece. Sensing his presence, she lifted her head. "Caspion!" Her light-brown eyes shimmered behind her comical eyewear.

He opened his arms, and she ran into them. "I've missed you, Tina." He clasped her against him.

"How long were you gone?"

"Awhile," he said, finally releasing her.

She removed her goggles. "Let's have a drink out on the balcony." As they used to do. "You can tell me everything."

He followed her into the main area of her suite. A new framed piece of art—a pencil sketch of Trehan Daciano rendered by her hand—hung in a prominent place on the wall.

Sick of that vampire. Cas glanced from the portrait to Bettina, noting the pink in her cheeks and the light in her gaze.

She was . . . happy. The Prince of Shadow was actually making her happy.

From a bar area, she poured demon brew for Cas and a sweet wine for herself.

Drinks in hand, they headed out to her balcony. The moon was nearly full in the sky, its light beaming down over the fog that wisped through the medieval town.

That moonlit mist reminded him of the vampire. *What doesn't?*

This sleepy hamlet seemed so much smaller than Cas remembered it. *Why did I care what these demons think of me?* As if they mattered in the grand scheme of his life. Cas got more satisfaction from one of Mirceo's awed looks than he'd experienced when this entire fickle populace had cheered for him.

Cas would tell them all to go to hell in order to have his mate beside him. *If my mate could be true.*

Bettina sipped her wine. "I'm so glad you're back, Cas. A lot has happened over these weeks."

"Catch me up."

"Well . . ." She exhaled a breath. "It turns out Trehan believed *I* was the one who poisoned him—in order to save you. To be fair, I did hand him a goblet of wine that night, and I *had* threatened to poison him before." Not to mention that she designed poison rings. "Not long after you left, he and I reconciled and married."

Still despise that prick. "How do the Abaddonae feel about a vampire as their king?"

She tucked her dark hair behind her ear. "Well, you know . . . they saw him at the death matches, and . . ."

"They love him." Abaddon's motto was *Might makes right.* "Cas, *I* love him." She couldn't contain a beaming smile. "And he adores me."

"Why wouldn't he, Tina? Daciano doesn't deserve you."

Her brows drew together. "Cas . . ."

Changing the subject, he said, "Where's Salem?" Her insolent phantom bodyguard.

"He secretly tagged along with me into Dacia, then took off! Now he's loose somewhere in the kingdom."

"Gods help the Dacians."

"I know, right? Speaking of hidden kingdoms, we, uh, called a truce with the Vrekeners not long ago."

Cas's head snapped up. "What the hell? What did Raum say about this?" The grand duke of the Deathly Ones had eagerly turned over the dimension to Bettina.

"He wasn't thrilled, but when I explained things, he came around." Tilting her head, she asked, "Do you want to see him while you're here?"

Cas wasn't ready to face him yet. Maybe if he had a more solid footing in his life. *Am I mated? Am I not?* This limbo was maddening. "Don't change the subject. Tell me about the Vrekeners."

"So much has happened. The leader of the gang who attacked me was their *king*. After Trehan killed those assholes, a new ruler stepped up. Thronos Talos. His mate is a sorceress!"

Surprising. "She managed to get him to stand down?"

Bettina sipped her wine. "No, Thronos is a decent guy. I like him."

Cas's jaw slackened. She had detested and feared Vrekeners, every last one of them.

"The king who hurt me was the outlier," she said. "The rest aren't like him."

"That we know of." *Give them time.*

Moving away from that subject, she said, "Please tell me how long you were gone. I mean, technically."

He swigged his brew. "Five hundred years or so."

Now *her* jaw slackened. "Why would . . . how could you remain away that long?"

"Because that's what it took for me to accept everything that happened."

Confusion marked her expression. "It wasn't *that* bad!"

"I fought for my honor and the honor of our people. Then I lost. Spectacularly."

"For the love of gold, Caspion, he was so much older than you."

In a low tone, he said, "Not anymore."

She stilled. "You have to let go of your animosity against Trehan. He's my husband, and you're my dearest friend. I can't lose either of you."

"I don't see us mending fences." Even if he could ever forget the pain that vampire had delivered, Cas wouldn't want to be anywhere near a Daciano to remind him of Mirceo.

"Trey feels awful about how he treated you. He was under the influence of a serious toxin during that fight. Does that count for nothing?"

Cas shrugged.

"He even offered to give you his scry crystal"—*no longer an option*—"to make amends, but also in recognition of your stellar career."

As a tracker. Cas's hunt for her attackers had been the most important of his life, now never to be completed—because of bloody Trehan.

Realization hit: Not only had Trehan avenged Bettina, that Dacian had also avenged Cas's mate for the deaths of Mirceo's parents!

Really fucking sick of that vampire.

She laid her hand on his arm. "You'll have to put aside your anger if you want a future with Mirceo."

Cas stilled. "Trehan told you."

"Oh, Cas, is Mirceo truly yours? Could you and I both have found our mates?"

"Yes, he's mine."

"I admit I was surprised when I heard this. You were always with females, so I thought you were straight."

"I am. Or I was. I've never desired a male before, but with Mirceo . . ." Cas exhaled. "I am very much *not* straight. I've never desired anyone like I do him." He scrubbed a hand over his face. "It's like a fever."

"Have you attempted him?"

"No. I don't think he can be faithful. He doesn't understand commitment, is too young to enter into one." At that age, even Cas would've had difficulty, and he'd desired matehood.

"Have you let him drink from you? It can really bond two people." A secretive smile played about her lips.

Let? Not at first. "He's fed from me. You allow Trehan to drink from you?"

Her cheeks reddened. "Of course. He didn't at first because of the bloodtaking taboo, but now . . ."

"You like it?"

Over the rim of her glass, she said, "I think you know the answer to that question."

Even now Cas was overfull with blood, aching to be pierced. "But I don't relish the idea of Mirceo having full access to my memories." Cas longed to be attractive to his fated one, to appear forever strong and brave—the hero of old.

When he thought of the things Mirceo could see, sweat beaded his upper lip. "I couldn't stand pity from him. Of all the people in the worlds, not him."

The vampire's words echoed in his mind: *Perhaps you don't lack faith in* me. *Perhaps you lack faith in* you. Maybe so.

"I felt the same way," Bettina said. "I was horrified at the idea of a brave warrior like Trehan seeing what a coward I was when the Vrekeners attacked."

Cas scowled. "You were set upon by a gang of violent swordsmen!"

"I didn't say I was being rational about it. In any case, Trehan did see, and he *did* pity me. But it was more than that. He explained something very important to me."

"Tina, I don't think I can bear hearing words of wisdom from that leech right now."

She glared. "Language, demon. That's my husband you're talking about. Would you call Mirceo a leech?"

"Yes. Routinely."

She waved that away. "Trehan explained that when you love someone, you take on their pain as your own. Trehan *hurt* for me. Mirceo will hurt for you—especially since he'll relive your pain firsthand."

Could Mirceo ever love him? Was the vampire even capable of it? "Let's speak of something else. I have something to show you." He pulled the coins from his coat. "Mirceo and I collected a bounty."

Bettina's gaze grew laser-focused on the pouch. "Gold."

"Not just any gold." He handed it to her.

She opened it, gasping at the contents. "Holy shit! This is . . . this is dragon gold!" She gazed up at him. "That must've been some bounty."

"A tough one, yes." She tried to return the pouch, but he held up his palm. "Mirceo suggested we give it to you, and for once, I agreed with him."

"Thank you so much! Will you please bring him around, so I can thank him too?"

Cas glanced out over the town again. "I don't see that happening. He and I will most likely go our separate ways for a time."

"Do you really believe that?"

"I explained some things to him about demon matehood. Once Mirceo wraps his head around all the implications, that hedonist will cut and run. Trust me." Didn't matter how much Cas wanted more with Mirceo, he couldn't *will* the vampire to change—any more than he could *will* time to pass on Poly.

She chewed her lip, her brows drawn. *Hurting for me. Is my yearning so obvious?*

Cas hated that he'd made her pensive. She'd had far too many worries of her own. "I should be going."

"Where? How will I get in touch with you?"

He finished his cup. "I'll stop by again soon."

She hefted the sack of coins. "I could make a ring out of some of these for you to give Mirceo."

To signal a commitment? Cas shook his head. "A waste of good gold. . . ."

TWENTY-SIX

Miss me, sweetheart?" Mirceo said from behind Caspion. It was sunset on the fourth day.

The demon's shoulder muscles bunched. "You. Fucking. Child."

"I missed you too." He'd counted down the seconds till he could return, choking down blood mead, dealing with his ever-growing lust, and hardly sleeping. Over those nights, he'd hunted for the males who'd hurt his mate, stalking the plane of Abaddon as a deadly mist. But he'd discovered that Caspion had long since killed those fiends. "Let's agree never to part again—"

Caspion twisted around, his expression half wrathful, half wrecked. "You didn't do as you said you would. You didn't consider things. Or else you would not be here!"

"I've clearly arrived just in time." In fact, he'd arrived fifteen minutes ago to spy, half-tracing so Caspion couldn't detect his presence or scent. The big demon had been pacing with his hands in fists. That muscle in his clenched jaw had ticked.

Mirceo hadn't been the only one counting down the seconds. As he'd watched, Caspion had drawn back a fist, slamming it into the wall.

Voice hoarse, the demon said, "Why have you come back?"

To get claimed. Mirceo had prepared his body for Caspion, and he had a vial of lubricating oil in his pocket. "Tonight is the hunter's moon—incidentally, my mate and I are hunters—and I have a date with him." He'd decided to bond with his male over more than just pleasure. Mirceo would delight all of his demon's senses with food, spirits, and spectacle.

They would drink and be merry, celebrating the beginning of their lives together. After Caspion claimed him, Mirceo's anxiety wouldn't arise. Obviously.

Just don't look at his neck. Ignore your throbbing fangs. If he fed from Caspion right now, they'd both come, which wouldn't do. To drag the demon over the finish line tonight, Mirceo needed to keep him on the edge.

"This isn't a fucking game! I could kill you for this. Do you doubt my resolve?"

"No. Nor do I doubt mine. One more time: I don't want anyone but you." Even in their very first meeting, Caspion had revealed hints of vulnerability. After experiencing his mate's past, Mirceo knew why. The demon *did* lack faith in himself, would think himself unworthy of a prince. *I'll convince him otherwise tonight.* "I could have gone out for the last few nights and bedded others, but I had zero interest." *Keep things light.* "Though I do admit to masturbating like a fiend." He held up his palms. "I'm surprised I don't have blisters."

A low growl left the demon's lips as he clearly called up the mental image. Inhaling for calm, he released Mirceo.

"Admit it: you're relieved I came back." *He's falling for me.*

Mirceo had known it. Who could resist him when he turned on the charm?

"Part of me. The rest is too busy reading the writing on the wall."

Mirceo refused to get dragged into an argument. "Speaking of which . . . I believe you've added to your collection of holes. Since this place is now half mine, lay off." He tapped his chin. "But I do think we should reside in our clifftop villa most of the time."

Caspion seemed to be grinding his molars. "You're going to see my memories sooner or later. Until you do, you won't know me well enough to make this commitment. Something you witness could change your mind. I won't have you use that as an excuse in a few centuries to take some kind of *break*."

"You assume I haven't already dreamed of your past?" Whenever he'd managed to doze for a few moments, Mirceo had experienced even more memories, including the one of Caspion's match against Trehan.

Mirceo had relived every horror. The fractured bones . . . the iron spike breaking off in the back of his head, lodging into his brain . . . Caspion's own people cheering for a male he despised more than anything. . . .

Trehan had disgraced him in front of an entire society. How could the demon ever set aside his revenge? Even Mirceo had awakened from that dream with the need to rip out his uncle's throat.

Cross that bridge when we come to it. "Maybe I know you inside and out, Caspion. And here I stand."

The demon's expression was difficult to read, but Mirceo got the sense that he'd just passed some kind of test. "I'm giving you one last chance to leave my presence." Caspion sidled closer, looking at him . . . differently.

Was the demon sizing Mirceo up sexually? *For the love of gods, let him be sizing me up sexually!* "Leave? Why would I do that? We're heading out on a date. I have a surprise destination for you."

Menace in his bearing, Caspion circled him. "You're pushing me too far, vampire."

Mirceo pivoted to keep him in sight. "As you asked of me, I considered all the ramifications of this relationship. Now *you* will do as *I* ask."

"What are you talking about?"

"Tonight you'll treat me like your mate, holding nothing back. Anytime an impulse arises, you must surrender to it. Now, go get dressed. I'm taking you out to celebrate in advance."

The demon's blond brows drew together. "Celebrate what?"

Mirceo laughed. "Didn't you hear? I'm getting marked tonight."

~

Cas fumbled to lace his pants, his nerves shot.

Taking on a legion of Wendigos? A walk in the park. But this . . .

He would soon claim his mate. Forever.

Cas had stopped trying to resist the irresistible, to deny the undeniable. At last, he would lose his demon seal, and he'd be experiencing that turning point—with his best friend.

After he'd changed into his fine leather breeches and an embroidered tunic—demon formalwear—he returned to the deck. Mirceo was gazing out at the sea, his heartbreaking face lit by the full hunter's moon.

Emotions rocked Cas, that tenderness returning a thousandfold. *Mine.*

Mirceo turned to him with his devil-may-care grin, lean

and sexy in his thin leather trench and pants that molded to his every muscle. No shirt, naturally.

But Mirceo's grin faded. "Gods almighty. I'm going to burst with pride to be on your arm tonight."

Cas, no stranger to others assessing his looks, felt his cheeks heating. His blush reminded him: "Do you not want to . . . drink from me?"

The vampire rubbed his tongue over a fang. "I'll wait till you claim me to enjoy my feast."

Mercy! How the hell could Cas make it through their *date?* When Mirceo had spoken earlier of getting marked, Cas had almost seized the vampire then and there.

"As fine as you are, demon, you need an accessory." Mirceo pulled something from his coat, tossing it to Cas.

A black domino?

Mirceo donned a similar one. The color emphasized the ring of onyx around his gray irises. *As if that perfect creature needs any embellishment.* "I scored us invitations to *the* masquerade of the Accession, demon. But you have to promise me we will stay till the clock strikes midnight."

"An *erotic* masquerade, no doubt. How could this be a good idea?"

"You'll see my attention is fixed solely on you—despite all the action around us. I've still got to get you to the finish line, and my obvious obsession with you should make this a lock."

Cas had to admire his determination—no matter how misguided his agenda. With a long-suffering exhalation, he tied on the mask. "Must we do this?"

Mirceo took his elbow. "We must." He traced them into a misty garden.

An opulent palace stood not far away. Lazy strains of music filtered through the night. "Where are we?"

"The most exclusive new pleasure den in the Lore. Come on." Mirceo linked arms with him.

Cas hesitated, feeling out of his element, but then Mirceo laughed at his reaction—*love that vampire's laugh*—and he began to relax.

They strolled toward the grand entrance, where liveried servants collected Mirceo's invitation. He and Cas stepped into an enormous ballroom packed with masked immortals of all different species.

The torchlit area was a riot of colors. Decadence seemed to be the theme. Giant nude statuary lined the walls. A swimming pool had been constructed in the middle of the ballroom floor. Water nymphs frolicked in its depths, descending upon any who entered.

Scantily clad fey performed on a high wire above. A female fire-eater and a male fire-breather made an erotic duo on a spotlighted stage.

All around them revelers raised hell. In the years approaching an Accession, any party could be an immortal's last, so they tended to make the most of them.

The dazzling displays lit up Cas's senses. Whenever he was near the prince, everything felt intense, his emotions—and instincts—amplified.

As he and Mirceo made their way through the crowd, attendees turned to stare. The vampire's sexual magnetism—and shirtless chest—commanded gazes from males and females alike.

Even over the din, Cas could hear their hearts speeding up as the prince passed. Many seemed to be conjecturing whether Cas and Mirceo were lovers.

When Cas caught a couple of demons scoping out Mirceo's

pale neck—checking for a claiming bite—he took Mirceo's hand in his own, delighting the vampire. Part of him longed to whisk Mirceo away where no one could see him. Part of him needed to show off the prince, to let everyone here know who Mirceo belonged to.

Does he belong to me? The vampire had returned, despite knowing the risk: eternal monogamy. And Mirceo had made it sound as if he'd already seen Cas's shaming memories—but they obviously hadn't tempered his regard.

How can I fight this? The prince was too mesmerizing to resist.

Drinks flowed from a gurgling champagne fountain. Blood mead and demon brew were on tap as well. Mirceo snagged two chalices, handing one to Cas. "What should we drink to?"

"To the bottom," Cas answered, making him grin. They finished their drinks and grabbed a couple more.

"Don't forget: you must follow all your impulses." Mirceo drained his cup, then reached for another one. "Now, get merry."

He had the impulse to please Mirceo, so up went Cas's goblet. The vampire was quick to hand him yet another.

A sinking realization set in. No matter what Cas chose to do, he was fucked. Separation from Mirceo delivered pain; nearness did the same—because at every second, he felt more and more how well Mirceo fit him. Whenever they were together, Cas comprehended what he would lose if the vampire bolted.

As he'd done on Poly, Cas would have to let go, to simply take the pain and accept his lot. For better or worse, he would claim the male as his own.

"What musings hide behind those blue eyes?" Mirceo asked.

"Thoughts of the future."

"Hmm. Can we not enjoy the present?"

Cas adjusted his mask self-consciously. "I am trying, Mirceo."

The vampire gazed up at him. "I know you are, love. And that means a lot to me." His sensual lips curled, spellbinding Cas. "Come on, I'm keen to show you off. . . ."

Over the next couple of hours, Cas fell even deeper under Mirceo's thrall. In a daze, he followed the tantalizing vampire through the party. Whatever vintage of brew Mirceo chose for Cas, he drank without hesitation. Whatever Mirceo hand-fed him, he obediently ate, sucking clean the vampire's elegant fingers.

Mirceo continued to tease him without mercy. In front of everyone, he reached up and traced the shape of Cas's sensitive horns. Grazing, petting, fondling them—till Cas thought his knees would buckle. "My magnificent demon," Mirceo rasped. "I'm so hard for you." Later, as they watched a bawdy skit, the vampire worked his hand into Cas's front pocket, slicing the leather open with a claw. Stretching his thumb through the opening, Mirceo rubbed Cas's frenulum till pre-cum flowed.

Each time Cas thought he could take no more, Mirceo would laugh and move on to the next sight or sensation. *Maddening me!*

Horns flaring obscenely, Cas warned him, "You're playing with fire."

Mirceo grinned. "Good, I like the burn."

Tunnel-visioned Cas couldn't see anything but his mate. He felt like a slavering beast chasing a butterfly.

And like a beast, Cas wanted to devour every inch of Mirceo's body. To make love to him. As his gaze roamed along the vampire's throat, his fangs sharpened to leave their mark.

Mirceo traced them to a deserted balcony. The voyeuristic vampire often liked to observe debauchery from a vantage point.

Guiding Cas to sit on a couch, Mirceo settled himself across his lap with casual ease, as if they'd been a couple for millennia.

Mirceo removed his mask, then untied Cas's. Together, they drank and watched other couples kissing and stroking each other.

Mirceo said, "You keep questioning my commitment, but do *you* miss hunting for a partner among all these beauties?"

Cas shook his head. When a lock of Mirceo's jet-black hair tumbled over his forehead, he reached for it, rubbing the silky texture between his thumb and forefinger. In a gruff tone, he admitted, "I have a hard time even seeing others when you're around." *Said the beast to the butterfly.*

"Good answer," Mirceo said. "It's difficult to believe that you and I are here together. From my first glimpse of you, I lusted for more."

"When did you know your feelings ran deeper?"

Mirceo blinked. "Deeper?"

Cas thumped his ear. "Prick."

The vampire laughed.

Must taste those lips. The urge was undeniable. He leaned in and nipped Mirceo's fuller bottom one, teasing the seam of them with his tongue. Threading his fingers through soft, black hair, Cas pulled him closer.

He took Mirceo's mouth; he claimed it with a lover's kiss. *I need you so fucking much. I'll be good to you, vampire. Just don't hurt me. Though so many have tried, only you have the power to destroy me. . . .*

When Cas drew back, Mirceo's lids were heavy, his lips reddened. "This will be over before it starts, demon. I've never wanted anything as I want you."

"And you always get what you want."

"Maybe. But tonight, my wonderful friend, *you* are going to get what you *need*."

"There's no turning back after this, Mirceo." As if they hadn't already crossed the threshold. This next step had been inevitable since the day each had been born for the other.

"I understand. Speaking of which, do you have any qualms about fucking a male?" He took Cas's hand, raising it to his mouth to suck the forefinger. Mirceo's wicked tongue flicked it, wetting it. Then the vampire placed that finger at his nipple.

Cas's breaths shallowed as he rubbed the hardened nub. "While you were passed out the other night, I explored your body, aching for everything I saw. I'll show you how much tonight." He gave a light pinch.

Mirceo went heavy-lidded. "Ah, so you're officially bisexual. Now *your* desires aren't as restricted."

"On the contrary. I'm not attracted to anyone but you."

The vampire gave him a knowing look. "Lots of people are Mircexual. You are not alone."

Mircexual? Cas's lips twitched. One thing he knew for certain—it would never be dull with this prince.

"Are you curious about spending? Demon, it's so fucking good. Your balls get so heavy and sore."

"I try to imagine what it will feel like." Reality hit Cas. *I'm going to spend my seed inside Mirceo's body. Soon.* "And you? Any qualms about what I'm going to do to you?"

Voice going low, Mirceo said, "Want to know a secret, sweetheart?"

His tone made Cas's heartbeat speed up even more. "When you ask me like that, I'm not entirely sure."

TWENTY-SEVEN

P laying with fire.

The demon had warned him, but Mirceo continued to push, waiting for the moment when his mate could no longer deny them what they both desperately needed.

He straddled Caspion, settling over the demon's stiffened cock. Mirceo's own shaft was so hard that the crown breached the waistband of his pants. "You'll want to know this secret." He leaned in to nuzzle Caspion's neck, lazily licking and sucking his skin. The demon's scent was all leather, his hectic pulse point teasing Mirceo's tongue.

Unable to resist, he grazed a fang along his mate's throat, drawing forth hot crimson. He moaned, "Your taste makes me insane."

Caspion's claws dug into his hips. "That's your secret? Kind of figured that out." The demon rocked him over his big rod, and Mirceo's ass ached for it.

"Oh, yes. My secret . . . Even when I knew we were fated, I never *craved* being fucked per se. I wanted it because I believed it would bond us. But over the last few nights, I began to prepare myself for your size, and things changed. . . ."

Looking enraptured, the demon said hoarsely, "Prepare?"

"With lubricant and toys to open myself up for you."

Caspion's shaft jerked. "Gods, the visual . . ."

"The sensations were mind-blowing." Mirceo grasped his hand again, sucking on the demon's thumb, wetting it. Then Mirceo placed it on the bared crown jutting from his pants.

Caspion's lips parted as he began to make slow, slick circles.

Could come just from that . . . "And when I pretended *you* were sinking into my ass"—he leaned forward to whisper at Caspion's ear—"my seed shot up over my chest, over my face, all the way to the headboard."

The demon jolted. "Come with me." Tracing to stand, he settled Mirceo on his feet, then snatched his hand. *"Now."*

Mirceo had been testing the demon's restraint; it seemed the bow had broken.

Caspion started dragging him down the stairs, then through the crowd, all the while scanning their surroundings.

Searching for a place to be alone? Mirceo almost wished he hadn't insisted on staying here until midnight. "So domineering."

Caspion paused, turning on Mirceo, that toe-curling demonic aggression at the fore. "Yes, I am." *And now I know why, love.* "Do you have a problem with that?"

"Does this look problematic, sweetheart?" He gestured to indicate his straining shaft, the head and a few inches protruding from his low-slung pants.

Caspion reached forward and cupped him with a proprietary grip. *"Mine."*

Mirceo bucked to his hand. "Not yet. But it will be. Cross the finish line with me?"

Curt nod. He began dragging Mirceo along again, plowing through the crowd.

No one in this packed masquerade could doubt what was about to happen to Mirceo. What a pair he and Caspion made.

A vampire with his dick hanging out and a catshifter-ate-the-canary smirk—and a demon with wild, obsidian eyes, baring his sharpened fangs at anyone who got in their way.

Every muscle in Caspion's towering frame bulged, and his horns jutted lewdly. More than one titillated female fanned herself as she gaped at them.

When he and Mirceo came upon a hallway, Caspion yanked open the first door, tearing it off its hinges. The fire in him seemed to have become an *inferno.*

Inside the room a saddled centaur cavorted with two nymph partners. One female rode him while he rode the other. Instead of a pommel, the saddle had a dildo. Each time the centaur bucked, the riding nymph would slip up and down.

The females called, "Mirceo!"

With a jealous growl, Caspion yanked him along.

They headed farther down the hallway, trying another door. The dimly lit chamber was empty. Smooth sheets covered the large, luxurious bed, and flames danced in the fireplace.

Caspion pushed him inside, then locked the door behind them.

So much was on the line that Mirceo suddenly grew . . . nervous. Not about losing his anal virginity, but what if he *wasn't* Caspion's?

What if I fail to please him? Mirceo nearly winced. *What if he has to think of females to stay hard?*

The demon grasped his face with reverent hands, leaning in to take his mouth again. With each lash of their tongues, Mirceo's senses swam, his doubts fading.

Caspion licked a fang to draw forth blood. As Mirceo moaned at the delectable taste, the demon slowly tongued Mirceo's mouth to feed him.

Sharing a blood kiss? *Hot, demon, filthy hot.* Mirceo drank in Caspion's groans, sucking on his pointed tongue. Greedy for more blood. More pleasure.

More demon.

～

Some long-dormant part of Cas seemed to be waking for this male. Clamoring. He couldn't deny such a primal pull—not when his heart yearned for the prince just as feverishly.

He took Mirceo's mouth until they were breathing for each other, until he got lost in bliss. Between kisses, they tore at one another's clothes. . . .

Cas surfaced from the daze when their bared cocks brushed. They'd already stripped? He drew back. "You've teased me all night. Got me in a lather." He ordered Mirceo, "On the bed with you. Now."

The prince flashed a devilish grin. "As you wish." He traced, then reclined upon the covers, his muscles taut with readiness. "I'll try to take it easy on my old man tonight."

Cas had begun to recognize the difference between Mirceo's genuine humor and the façade that masked his emotions. Right now, he could tell that the unflappable Prince of Dacia was *nervous.*

The sound of his mate's hammering heartbeat brought on another wave of tenderness in Cas. "I'm not going to hurt you, Mirceo."

"I trust you." The vampire's gray eyes turned onyx as he took in Cas's body. "Gods, I love all that tanned skin and golden hair. My fair-haired Adonis. No male has a more glorious mate than I."

"Agree to disagree."

"Ah, you like what you see, demon?" Sly, seductive vampire.

Cas gave a nod. *Mine.* "Spread your legs."

Brows raised, Mirceo did.

Cas knelt between them, gazing down at Mirceo's generous cock, at the beading tip. Seizing the shaft in his fist, he struggled to pace himself—to *not* fall upon his mate in a frenzy. He leaned down and nuzzled Mirceo's balls, inhaling his mate's drugging scent: *pure sex.*

Mirceo groaned. "You don't have to suck me, demon." His accent was thicker than Cas had ever heard it.

"*Have* to? I'm ravenous for you, mate." He kissed Mirceo's glistening cockhead, eagerly sampling its cream.

The prince jerked and moaned.

When the taste of Mirceo's pre-cum registered, Cas rasped, "Sometime tonight I'll drink your seed, drink it down." Never taking his eyes from Mirceo's, he circled his pointed tongue around the broad head. It was so taut and smooth. So *alive.* He smoothed his lips over the swollen tip, flicking it till the vampire exhaled a ragged breath.

"Gods almighty!" Mirceo eased up on an elbow to watch, the corded ridges of his torso rippling. "Want to see your gorgeous face." He brushed Cas's hair back. Whatever Mirceo saw in his expression made the vampire's heart race even faster.

As Cas sealed his lips over the head and sucked him down to the hilt, Mirceo breathed, "Ah, fuck me."

Cas gave a harsh groan around the prince's thick rod. *Soon.*

"Y-you're sure you've never done this?"

He drew back, meeting Mirceo's gaze. "I excel at my every endeavor."

The vampire thumped Cas's forehead. "Smart ass."

When Cas set back in with a grin, Mirceo drew his knees up, subtly thrusting as he cradled the back of Cas's head. The vampire's thighs quaked around his ears. *Already close.*

He savored Mirceo's reactions. The low rumbly sounds he made. The way he struggled to hold out as Cas's mouth and throat engulfed his length. His heels digging in as he rocked his hips.

When Cas splayed his fingers under Mirceo, the vampire's ass writhed in his palms. *I'm going to claim this ass tonight.* Overcome, Cas sank his claws into pale flesh, clutching his mate closer.

TWENTY-EIGHT

It's the demon's first time; want him to love this.

But for a first-time effort, Caspion was sending Mirceo off his axis, deep-throating while suckling with greedy pulls.

"You're devouring me!" Unable to restrain himself, Mirceo grabbed his mate's sensitive horns, bucking to his lips and grinding against his tongue.

"Uhn!" Caspion's muscles tensed, his big body wracked with demonic lust.

"Can't last much longer!" Mirceo teetered on the razor's edge. When the demon fondled his balls, he yelled, "Do you want my cum?"

Caspion drew back, releasing him, leaving Mirceo's shaft wet and pulsing against his belly. "I do. But you're not to spend yet."

Mirceo blinked for focus "What?" He let go of his mate's horns, saying, "Fuck that." His hand dipped, and he grasped his length. "I'm about to explode!"

Caspion seized his wrists, growling, "That cock belongs to me." He bared his sexy fangs. "Take your fucking hands off it."

Mirceo's shaft jerked from the command. *Never been so hard!* "*Now*, mate."

Somehow he released his grip. To combat the temptation, Mirceo let his arms fall over his head. "There." His body quaked from the denied release. "I-I surrender."

Caspion's gaze raked over him. "Look at you. You are *mine*." He fisted his hand in Mirceo's hair, tugging. "Say my name."

"*Caspion.*"

"I'm goin' to fuck you till you scream it." The demon leaned forward to suck an earlobe. "Till everyone here knows who makes you come."

Mirceo gasped at those words.

"But first I need to get my treasured mate ready." In bed, Caspion was a mix of pure demon filthiness and heartrending sweetness.

"There's a vial of oil in my pocket," Mirceo said, though Caspion's distended cock was producing so much pre-cum they might not need it. The head brushed against Mirceo's thigh, leaving a distinct trail of dampness.

The demon retrieved the vial and returned. "Spread your thighs wider for me." He poured oil on his fingers, then reached between Mirceo's legs. "Don't be nervous."

Mirceo glanced away with a smirk. "Wouldn't any blushing virgin be?"

"Ah-ah. Don't do that."

"What?"

"Give me the face you give others. I want all of you. The real you."

Mirceo swallowed thickly. With the demon staring down at

him, he felt exposed. Raw. Somehow he forced himself to hold Caspion's gaze. Words left his lips. "Demon, I'm glad it's you."

"I'm going to take care of you, Mirceo. Tonight and always." Caspion grazed his slick forefinger between Mirceo's cheeks, scarcely making contact with that needy part of him.

Each pass of his finger, the demon applied a bit more pressure, hard enough to breach him, just barely.

Mirceo's groan of frustration made Caspion hiss in a breath. "My greedy boy wants more?" With one hand gripping a hip to hold Mirceo steady, Caspion circled the pad of his finger.

Circling... circling... Mirceo moaned at the exquisite sensations.

Then the demon dipped inside to his second knuckle.

At last! "More, more!" *So much better than a toy.*

Caspion pumped his finger. "Always." More oil. Deeper penetration. Another finger joined the first, wedging inside, stretching. "You're going to be so tight around me."

The demon thrust those fingers just enough to get Mirceo ready—while keeping him on the brink. For what felt like agonizing hours, he gave shallow pumps.

More oil. *Deeper.* More oil. *Wider.*

Panting, Mirceo said, "I-It feels unreal. One night you'll have to let me fuck you too."

Caspion nodded easily. "Of course."

You'd give me control? "Even though you're dominant?"

Brows drawn, he answered, "What could be more dominant than providing my mate every pleasure he covets?"

Mirceo's chest twisted for this male. His heart felt overfull from emotion—yet without an outlet. They shared a look.

I don't know what to say, can't express how much I want you. This really will be forever. I'm falling for you, demon.

Caspion rasped, *"I know. I know.* I feel the same way."

Yes, Mirceo's heart was overfull—but every inch of his body felt empty, receptive to whatever the demon wanted to give him. By the time Caspion removed his fingers, Mirceo was insensible, shamelessly rolling his hips. *"Pleasepleaseplease, demon."*

Caspion knelt between his legs and squirted more oil. To slather over that heavy length? Mirceo shot upright to behold his golden demon oiling himself. He was transfixed as Caspion glided a big hand over his cock—across the taut crown, the thickened base, along those prominent veins.

"Wanted you for so godsdamned long, Mirceo." Had the demon's horns ever been so straight and swollen? "Do you trust me not to hurt you?"

"I do. I trust you in this. I trust you in everything. I always have."

Biceps bulging, Caspion clamped Mirceo's hips and dragged him closer. Then he fisted his length. When the broad head tucked against Mirceo's entrance, the demon groaned as if in anguish; Mirceo cried out, shaking from the contact.

As Caspion pressed the tip inside, he held Mirceo's gaze. "You are mine. Forever. I'll never let you go." Beginning to sweat, he inched forward, until the entire oiled crown had passed Mirceo's ring. "Ah! My mate's so fucking *tight.*"

Mirceo moaned because it was so good. Better than good.

Gnashing his teeth, the demon delved farther, his girth difficult to accept. Even so, pleasure suffused Mirceo the deeper Caspion went. Mirceo's own shaft jutted above his belly like a steel rod. He feared it would go off without a touch.

"Waited five hundred years for this." Caspion withdrew a couple of inches and peered down, gaze riveted to where their bodies joined. *If eyes could incinerate . . .*

As Mirceo writhed, trying to adjust, the demon drizzled more oil. "Don't fight me," he bit out. "Let me in."

When Mirceo willed himself to relax as much as he could, Caspion sank farther inside, his rigid length stretching Mirceo, forcing him to yield.

"That's it! Vampire . . . everything I can do not to come!" His brows were drawn, his mighty chest heaving as his fingers dug into Mirceo's hips. He was stronger, demonic, older, and he was *impaling* Mirceo—yet Caspion seemed overpowered. *"Want deep inside your virgin ass."*

The demon got his wish. Deeper. Deeper. *Deep,* until Caspion had filled him with thick, pulsating flesh. *"Mine!"* he roared in triumph.

With a mindless yell, Mirceo surrendered . . . everything.

～

Don't come . . . don't come . . . gods, don't come.

Nothing in Cas's life could have prepared him for this lust. He'd been on the verge from the moment his cockhead had kissed Mirceo's entrance. He ignored the tingling in his spine, the heavy ache in his balls. *Won't come before my mate.*

He burned to wrest more pleasure from the vampire than anyone ever had before, to be the only one Mirceo fantasized about. *Just don't come.* "I've possessed you. Completely." He sounded crazed. "I'm inside your body. I'll always be a part of you." He drew back his hips and thrust—

Found paradise. His eyes rolled back in his head. *My home. This vampire's my home.*

When Cas grew aware of his surroundings again, Mirceo was still arching his back like a bow, his shaft bouncing between them.

Cas's gaze widened. "What was that?"

"Do it again! You're hitting my prostate." Mirceo's cock had painted his pale torso with pre-cum.

Awestruck, Cas slowly withdrew, then inched back in.

"Right . . . right *THERE*!" Mirceo's head thrashed. "Want this always. You inside me. NEED it."

Sweating, Cas sank in just enough to rub the vampire right at that spot.

Mirceo bit his lip so hard that blood ran down his chin. *My stunning vampire mate.* Cas leaned down and licked the stream, then took Mirceo's mouth to feed it to him.

Their tongues tangled as Cas drew his hips back, then rolled them forward. *Don't come, don't come!* After another measured stroke, he fucked harder, grunting.

His sweat-slicked body slapped the oiled curves of Mirceo's ass—flesh that Cas had conquered completely. He broke from the kiss and raised himself on straightened arms. "No going back, vampire." Clenching his jaw, he dug his knees into the bed to thrust harder.

The prince's moan grew continuous. *He's on the edge.*

So was Cas. *Never felt pressure like this.* His cock throbbed with each of his heartbeats.

"About to come, demon! Can't last . . ."

Holding the vampire's gaze, he said, "Do you want my spend inside you?" His free hand trailed down his mate's belly.

Mirceo panted in anticipation. "Gods yes, give it to me, demon!"

"Then wring it from me," Cas commanded. "Take it from me with your tight little ass." He curled his oiled fingers around Mirceo's shaft. Right as he plunged, he stroked.

"My gods! Fuck, yes!" Mirceo's agonized expression

transformed to one of ecstasy. *"YES!"* His cock jerked, then began to spurt between them—would've caught Mirceo's face, if not for Cas's hand. *"DEMON!"*

He wrenched yells from Mirceo's lungs and cum from his rod. With each surging jet of seed, Mirceo's ass contracted all along Cas's length.

Cataclysmic. He gave a savage bellow. *"Fucking feel you!"*

Still coming, Mirceo yelled, "Mark me; do it!"

Cas's demonic gaze locked on the flesh of Mirceo's neck. *"Mine!"* He whipped his head forward and sank his fangs into his mate.

Marking him. Possessing him. Taking them past a boundary they could never return to.

Mirceo arched and writhed beneath him. *"YES, YES!"*

Cas snarled against the vampire's throat. With one brutal thrust, that throbbing pressure in his cock gave way.

As his demon seal vanished, Cas's eyes flashed open wide. *It's happening.* Erupting in a searing rush of semen, he claimed his mate forever. . . .

TWENTY-NINE

The vampire slept against his chest.

As Cas brushed Mirceo's silken hair from his spellbinding face, his demon instincts were at rest.

My mate is with me. Happy. Healthy. Safe.

Claimed. Cas was ready to seize their destiny together—whatever that might bring.

He'd told Mirceo, *May the gods help any pups with you as a father,* but now his opinion had changed. After all, Mirceo had already raised one child: Kosmina. He was strong, and he was fun—pups would adore him. *I should be so lucky to raise a family with him.*

Cas would provide the structure, Mirceo the heart.

And while biological offspring had once seemed so important, couldn't he and the vampire raise some foundlings as well?

Cas's lips curved. *Why have I never considered that before . . . ?*

For the first time in his existence, he comprehended what peace felt like. Basking in it, he pressed a kiss to Mirceo's hair and inhaled his scent.

The staggering surprise of what ejaculating felt like had been nothing compared to the bond he shared with the vampire. Cas had accepted his ungodly need for this male. Embraced it. Surrendered to it.

The hours they'd just indulged in each other had played out like a fever dream. Another two bouts in the bed and one in the shower had introduced Cas to fantasies he'd never known he'd had.

Now he relived snapshots of a night forever burned into his memory. *His exquisite mate riding him, sucking blood from Cas's finger, taking his demon seed again . . . Mirceo spilling his own semen upon Cas's tongue . . . the prince bellowing into the pillow as Cas mounted him from behind.*

Their shower together had been no less life-altering. *Mirceo slipping behind him under the cascade, teasing him to distraction . . . Cas planting his palms on the tiled wall, offering his ass . . . Mirceo gripping his horns to drag Cas's head back—right as the vampire bottomed out . . .*

Fangs piercing. Tile buckling under a demon's frenzied grip. Spontaneous cum lashing the wall . . .

This night—somehow both wicked and beautiful—had changed them forever.

Cas's lust was rekindling, but his young mate slept soundly. Mirceo obviously needed to rest. Hell, their separation for the last few days had taken its toll even on an older demon like Cas.

His lids grew heavier. But just as he drifted off, a stray question whispered through his consciousness.

Will the vampire be here when I open my eyes once more?

THIRTY

Mirceo woke with his claws digging into his own chest, a low whine ringing in his ears. His own?

Caspion slept beside him, spooning him securely in his brawny arms. *Heaven.* So why did Mirceo feel such anxiety?

No! Everything had gone perfectly last night. He'd gotten his dearest wish. When he'd fallen asleep against Caspion, he'd been secure in the knowledge that he and his mate were going to have a remarkable future together.

The low roil of panic he'd always experienced after sex hadn't disappeared; it'd escalated! His thoughts were in chaos. *Maybe I want him too much.*

Intense pain radiated in his left arm, just below the shoulder. He craned his head around but didn't see any bruising or injury. The rest of his body felt amazing.

So what the hell was wrong with him? Could a panic attack manifest itself as phantom pain in a limb?

He glanced back at Caspion's sleeping face, and a pang momentarily overrode his panic.

I . . . I . . .

Why couldn't Mirceo complete the thought? *I . . .*

Desire him? *Not news.* Want him for all time? *Again, not news.* Need him? *Obviously.*

Easing out of Caspion's embrace, he traced to his feet. As he dragged on his pants, Mirceo struggled to marshal his scattered thoughts. Maybe he truly hadn't been ready to promise his entire future. Had he made a deal with the devil to get what he wanted? And now that devil would collect on his soul?

But if he suffered from commitment doubts, then why was his heart telling him to stay close to Caspion? Shouldn't he be running away? And why hadn't he experienced anything like this during his other encounters with the demon?

Mirceo traced to one of the draped windows, peeking out. The orange hunter's moon hung low, setting over the grounds. The sun would soon rise.

As he stared, he felt as if he'd missed something he should have noticed—the feeling akin to that frustrating sense when a word is on the tip of one's tongue but can't be called forth. He began to pace beside the bed. *What am I forgetting . . . ?*

In time, Caspion stirred. The demon woke with a smile, blinking open those blue eyes. With his first look at Mirceo, his breathtaking smile faded. "Oh, for fuck's sake, vampire."

"What?"

He sat up, raking tousled blond hair off his forehead. "You *know* what. You've already checked out."

"I haven't said a word." Sweat beaded his forehead and upper lip. Mirceo didn't *sweat* unless he exerted himself during sex.

"You don't have to; your wild-eyed expression is saying everything."

Saying what? *Explain it to me! Make me understand.*

Caspion rose to snatch his clothes off the floor. "Knew this would happen."

Even now the sight of that physique had Mirceo hardening. *What wouldn't I have promised to possess him?* "What does my expression say?"

Caspion grated, "It's—been—swell." He stabbed his legs into his pants.

"You're putting words in my mouth."

"I knew you'd do this!" His instincts must be going crazy. Just as a demon would need to claim his fated one, he wouldn't tolerate losing a marked mate. Yet Caspion was clearly trying not to lose his temper. "I knew. But you convinced me to take a chance."

"Since we are mated, I thought I wouldn't feel this . . . this . . ."

"Regret?"

"Not regret." Mirceo examined his emotions. "I don't feel any regret."

"You never regretted your conquests. Just the mornings after. Damn you, I told you to take time. To be certain."

"I know."

"You promised me eternity, and you didn't even make it eight fucking hours! You told me things would be different with me, with your mate."

"It *is* different. My anxiety is stronger than it's ever been." *Why am I provoking him?*

"You prick." Caspion inhaled a deep breath, making another valiant attempt to control his rising anger. "Look, I understand this is a lot to process. What happened between us was mind-boggling. We're both emotionally raw and charged up right now. But we have something here. Don't throw it all away."

The calmer Caspion managed to remain, the more agitated

Mirceo grew. "Throw it all away? Is that on the table?" *Make this feeling stop!*

"You want it to be?"

"No. *No!*"

"Last night spooked the hell out of me too, and I'm in a place in my life where this is perfect timing. For you, the timing couldn't be worse. But if you can trust me, we will make it work."

That pain in Mirceo's arm wouldn't let up. He scowled down at it.

"Are you even listening to me?" Caspion demanded. "What occurred between the time you fell asleep and the time you woke up?"

"That's what I'm trying to tell you: I don't know! Maybe . . . maybe I should go away for a couple of days and get my mind in order—"

"No. You made a decision; abide by it. If you leave here this morning, then you leave for good."

Leave for good. Leave *Caspion*. Mirceo's alarm ratcheted up even more.

The demon narrowed his eyes. "You dreamed a memory of mine, didn't you? I can guess which one." His face flushed, even as his eyes filled with bitterness.

Mirceo wanted to say, *Your memories have nothing to do with what I'm experiencing.* But that might be a lie. When he thought of how those demons had mistreated his young mate, his insanity only seemed to peak.

"No denial. So you *have* dreamed my memories. And you're saying they aren't affecting you?"

"They are. Just not the way you assume." Mirceo couldn't untangle his thoughts. This strangling sensation wouldn't relent. He pinched his temples, fearing he was about to pass out from lack of oxygen. "I-I haven't made any decisions or anything."

"That's worse! After last night, how could you decide on anything other than *more?*"

"Do you think I *want* to feel like this?" His emotions weren't just strangling Mirceo, they were breaking over him like a tsunami and crushing him. Drowning him. "What is this? Tell me!" Mirceo hadn't lost interest—just the opposite. He wanted this male even more desperately than before. "Help me, Caspion. *Please.* Because I think . . . I think I'm losing my mind."

"You're panicked because you don't want your hedonistic life to change." Caspion scrubbed a hand over his face. "I've no one to blame but myself. I'm an idiot for trusting you. I know your faults—and I saw this coming."

That pissed Mirceo off. *I never saw it coming.* "That's not why I'm unraveling. You keep saying you know me, but maybe you don't." His head had begun to ache, a low throbbing over his brow.

"Bullshit!" Caspion pointed his forefinger at him. "I know you better than you know yourself."

The pain in Mirceo's head provoked his own anger. "You only think you do, demon. I have secrets."

"Such as?"

"The first night we met, I led you to believe we'd be nothing more than friends, but I was already plotting to fuck you."

"And now you have fucked me," Caspion said without shame.

Might as well do this now. "My friends wagered whether I could seduce the proud demon warrior—the conquest of all conquests."

"Friends? Those sycophants? *We* are friends, Mirceo. *They* are parasites. Is that the life you're in a hurry to get back to?"

"No!" Return to that superficial, dissolute world? Mirceo would rather live in that dismal cave with Caspion and fight Wendigos his whole life. *So why am I losing my mind right now?* "I just need to—to think about things for a time."

"You were supposed to think about things *before* we did this. What's done is done, vampire. And—as I warned you repeatedly—it can't be undone." His gaze rose to Mirceo's neck.

"Your mark." Mirceo's skin had healed, but demons would still be able to see it.

"You'll wear it forever. Does *that* panic you?"

"No, but something does." He felt as if he was about to vomit all the blood he'd taken last night.

~

"An endless supply of new partners will grow stale in time," Cas said. In a few centuries, once Mirceo figured out how meaningless his existence was, the vampire would attempt to find his mate. *But I'll be done.* He could never get over Mirceo's infidelity. The jealousy would eat him alive. "You will wish for a life with me, and I won't take you back."

When Mirceo rubbed his chest, comprehension dawned for Cas. "There's nothing I can say to calm your thundering heart right now, is there?"

The vampire remained silent. His color was pasty, his face waxen.

Cas felt like he could hold Mirceo here, guilting him into staying. *But if he doesn't want me . . . if he needs to flee so badly he looks sick . . .* "So now you're done with me? On to the next conquest? I'll be the latest in a long line, one among all the ruined souls you left in your wake." Grief seeped into him. "Do you even care that the people you bed begin to dream?" *Damn it, I began to dream of our future!* "Just as I predicted, you've lost interest."

Mirceo paced, sweating even more. "I-I haven't lost interest in you."

Ah, so the greedy prince wanted Caspion—*and* others. Perhaps he'd always planned for that, carrying on the lifestyle they'd had before, but sharing a bed as well. "You mentioned secrets, leech. You might as well clear the air completely."

He shook his head hard. "Don't think that's a good idea."

Now Cas definitely had to hear whatever Mirceo concealed. He traced in front of him, prodding the vampire's chest. "Tell me."

Mirceo stumbled backward until he met the wall. "M-my thoughts aren't right." Agitation and confusion warred in his expression. He swallowed loudly. "We should talk later—"

"NOW."

Gaze darting, Mirceo blurted, "I paid those three nymphs to manipulate us into kissing."

"What???" That night had rerouted the course of Cas's entire life!

Mirceo's eyes widened, as if he'd never intended to say those words. He muttered a vile curse in Dacian.

"You set me up?" Cas's hand had been forced yet again by this devious vampire. *Taking away my choice!* His fists clenched. "You fucking child. You played with my life. With my mind."

"I-I did. I regret my actions, but I admit them."

"You're telling me this to force me to leave. Because you're too big of a coward to walk away! Guess what? It's working—"

"No!" Mirceo traced to the room's wastebasket. Dropping to his knees, he vomited blood.

Cas's first impulse was to care for his mate—which infuriated him even more. "Look at you! Your body's told us all we need to know."

Mirceo swiped his arm over his mouth, then rose unsteadily to his feet.

Resentment seethed inside Cas. He burned to share his new

pain, to make the vampire feel a fraction of this agony. "Before I go, there's something you should know. I lied too, leech. You did have much to do with my stay on Poly. I suspected we had some tie, but I didn't *want* it. I didn't want *you*. I preferred to remain in that godsforsaken wasteland than be with you. Makes sense—my instincts were trying to protect me from a spoiled, degenerate princeling with no purpose, no resolve, and no fortitude."

Mirceo's expression grew stricken. Pressing his arm over his mouth, he fled, tracing away.

Cas gazed around the room, disbelieving he was alone. Then he threw back his head and roared.

THIRTY-ONE

As Mirceo paced the rooms in his clifftop villa, time seemed to move in fast-forward.

The sun set. Night fell. Dawn appeared, only to intensify into noon. Dusk tiptoed in with the nearly full moon.

All the while he questioned his actions, his sanity. The panic only grew, as did that sense that he was missing some huge detail that should be foremost in his mind. Yet now these feelings competed with anguish over the estrangement from his mate.

He kept gazing around, as if Caspion would trace into this room, a hero to be worshipped, to save Mirceo from his own wretchedness. From his stupidity. His weakness.

Within minutes of their fight, Mirceo had been tempted to trace to the bungalow, but he'd feared he would just prove the demon's points. *You said I have no fortitude—behold! Resolve? Not here, lover.*

He scowled at his arm when that pain flared again. Maybe Mirceo was just losing his mind. He raised his flask, attempting to sip a concoction that was more mead than blood.

Damn it, he didn't want others, didn't want to move on to the next conquest. He wanted to tease and conquer Caspion every day and night for the rest of their lives.

So why hadn't Mirceo told him that? *Because I'm my own worst enemy.* Caspion had known that about Mirceo. *Why didn't I know it?*

Hours had passed into days, but Mirceo had gotten no closer to deciphering his feelings. He needed Caspion to help him. The demon was a brilliant male. If they worked together, they could come up with a solution. Mirceo believed in Caspion—even if the reverse wasn't true.

Would the demon even take him back? A degenerate princeling . . . ?

Deciding to beseech Caspion's forgiveness and help, Mirceo traced to the bungalow. *Please. I will try harder. I will do better. Don't give up on me.*

Caspion wasn't there. So Mirceo waited.

And waited. In those maddening hours, he haunted his mate's home like a ghost.

Inhaling the demon's scent on a pillow.

Staring at the blankets Caspion had strung up over the windows.

Gazing out at the shore where the demon had risen like a god.

Mirceo brushed his fingertips over the holes in the wall, murmuring, "I've caused him so much pain."

Caspion's words kept ringing in his ears: *You are your own worst enemy. . . .*

~

Two days had passed, but Caspion never returned.

Unable to remain still any longer, Mirceo traced to the Red Flag, heading to the bar.

"Have you seen Caspion?" he asked Leyak.

The demon frowned. "You look terrible, vampire. Bad breakup, huh?"

The barkeep hadn't been referencing a *hunting* partnership. "How could you tell we were together?"

"Looked like an invisible leash tied you two."

And then Mirceo had severed it. "Has he been in here?"

"Oh, aye. Looked worse than you do. Took a job in another dimension. A real dangerous one."

Nausea roiled. "I should be with him! Tell me where he is."

"Sorry, son. I can't do that. Caspion said you . . . played with him."

"Not intentionally! I didn't set out to hurt him. I acted like an idiot." He swiped his hand over his clammy face. "*Please* tell me where he is, Leyak. I can keep him safe. No one can protect him like I will. I need to be with my mate."

The demon shook his head. "I don't want you running after him, distracting him and getting him killed."

Maybe Mirceo should kidnap the barkeep and torture him for Caspion's location. Of course! But then he recalled his mate's memories of this demon. Leyak had always been kind and encouraging to Caspion, the first ever to take an interest in his wellbeing. *You stalked that trail like a Caspion tiger, son!*

Damn it! No torture, then.

Mirceo's gaze snapped to the wall. He remembered many of the posted jobs. Maybe he could determine which ones were missing.

The next-most-lucrative bounty was still in play. Below the painted image of a pretty, pointed-eared female were the details:

REWARD:
WANTED ALIVE!
NAME: UNKNOWN
SPECIES: FEY
HAIR: LONG, LIGHT BROWN
EYES: ONE AMBER, ONE VIOLET
HEIGHT: 5'4"
REWARD: A QUEEN'S RANSOM IN GOLD
OFFERED BY KING ABYSSIAN INFERNAS, RULER OF PAN-
DEMONIA AND ALL HELLS

A few posters were conspicuously missing, and Mirceo recalled the details of them as best he could. He'd go to the location of each one. *I will hunt the hunter....*

~

A week had passed, and Mirceo was no closer to finding Caspion.

There were only so many more places he could be. Mirceo returned to the tavern, hoping the barkeep would take pity on him and reveal Caspion's whereabouts.

Leyak *should* pity him. Mirceo's clothes hung off his gaunt frame. His skin was deathly pale. Earlier, he'd forced himself to drink, but the blood hadn't made a dent in his deficit.

As he headed to the bar, Mirceo passed the bounty wall. Out of the corner of his eye, he spied a poster that made his head jerk around.

Cold fear snatched his heart. His never-ending panic morphed into a deafening roar that burst from his lungs. His invisible arm injury flared, his legs buckling. On his knees, he vomited blood all over the floor.

This. I sensed THIS.

Unable to process what was happening, he somehow managed

to trace to Castle Dacia. *Caspion, I need you! Gods, I need my mate.* Inside the black-stone throne room, diamond-filtered sunlight beamed in through stained-glass windows. Upon a raised dais, Lothaire sat in his throne, Elizabeth close beside him in her own.

Everyone was here. Mirceo's uncles Viktor, Stelian, and Trehan. Even Balery. Was Elizabeth's expression pensive? Lothaire's red gaze seemed even eerier than usual.

Mirceo yelled at Lothaire, "What the fuck have you done?"

Lothaire laughed, a full-throated sound that carried through the court, wrapping around each of them like chains. "Whatever I please, boy. One of the perks of being a king."

And all the world went red. . . .

THIRTY-TWO

Take a job or go crazy. Take a job or go crazy.
For a male who despised being hemmed in, Cas's entire life had come down to two options. So he'd taken a job.

After ten days of work and a successful bounty, he returned to the Red Flag to select his next mission. Inside, the usual crowd drank. Leyak hummed while he wiped down the bar.

Cas crossed to the completed board to pin up his cashed-in bounty, unable to stop himself from glancing around the tavern with a tiny spark of hope.

No Mirceo. The vampire was doubtless back to form, enjoying the shadow life, nailing everything that moved.

He'd expected this separation to send his demonic instincts raging out of control, but far more than instinct was at work here. It seemed Cas's tenderness toward Mirceo influenced everything. Rage and aggression had morphed into raw grief.

Cas could try to move on. Find a demoness and start siring

pups. But he only wanted the vampire. When Mirceo had fled that morning, he'd taken Cas's heart with him.

Cas had traced from the palace directly to the beach bungalow, then remained there for almost two days, praying to all the gods that the vampire would realize his mistake.

Over that time, he'd imagined Mirceo begging for forgiveness and vowing that he could handle an eternal commitment—oh, and that he wouldn't vomit at the thought of fucking only Cas for the rest of his life.

Then he'd realized Mirceo wasn't coming for him. And luckily he couldn't find the vampire; else Cas would've stalked after him like a lovelorn fool.

He exhaled a defeated breath. *Take a job or go crazy.*

Leyak called, "Caspion, a word."

"Yeah." He traced to the bar, hoping the old hunter wouldn't grill him again about Mirceo. The last time, Cas had said only, "The vampire played with my head." But his anger over Mirceo's machinations and scheming had swiftly faded. If the two of them hadn't been mates, maybe his resentment would've lasted. Yet they *were* mates. Everything had led them together. . . .

Leyak poured him a mug of brew. "How're you hanging in there?"

"Been better." Cas would own his part in his and Mirceo's rift. If he had derived any wisdom—or discipline—from all the years he'd lived, he would've disappeared from the vampire's life for ten decades.

But Cas had been too weak to leave. Instead, he'd laid all of the choice, all of the *burden*, on such a young male. Then Cas had been shocked when Mirceo bolted in a panic?

That morning, the vampire's claw marks had studded his own chest. To judge by its beat, Mirceo's heart must've been on the verge of exploding. Cas understood that panic—he'd experienced the same when he'd rashly fled Dacia all those years ago, risking his own execution. But at that age, *rash* had felt *right.*

So it would with Mirceo.

Trying not to sound desperate, Cas asked, "I don't suppose he stopped by?"

"As a matter of fact, he came in a few times asking after you, wanting your location. Searched for you too."

Damn this surge of hope! "And?"

"He was here a couple of days ago, looking haunted-eyed and miserable."

Cas had pictured Mirceo, smirk in place, fucking and biting partners with abandon. Instead, the prince had been miserable? That shouldn't make Cas happy. But it did. A smile crossed his face. "Did he say if he was coming back?"

"Dunno. He saw something on the bounty wall and he . . . reacted."

"What do you mean?"

Leyak scratched one of his scuffed horns. "I mean, he dropped to his knees, roared in pain, and vomited blood. Which I will never get out of the floor."

Cas's claws dug into the bar. "What did he see?"

"I didn't catch the specific poster, but he didn't take it down or anything. Just teleported from here like a bat out of hell."

Cas traced to the board, scanning the bounties. His breath left him when a familiar portrait snared his attention. He'd once viewed that same likeness while sitting atop the tower of a mortal bridge.

Mina. *My sister-by-fate . . .*

REWARD:
MISSING!
NAME: PRINCESS KOSMINA
SPECIES: VAMPIRE
LAST SEEN: NEW ORLEANS RIVERFRONT, SETTING OF
THE HUNTER'S MOON
HAIR: LONG, LIGHT BLOND
EYES: BLUE
HEIGHT: 5'5"
REWARD: FATHOMLESS
OFFERED BY KING LOTHAIRE, THE ENEMY OF OLD

My sister! Cas yanked the poster down, rereading the details. The hunter's moonset? That'd been right when—

Dear gods, Mirceo had *sensed* his beloved sister was in danger!

Cas traced back to the bar. Holding up the poster, he demanded, "How did this get here?"

Leyak shook his head. "Came in through the usual channels."

I've got to get to Dacia. To Mirceo. His eyes narrowed. For a male who revered choice, Cas had only one option.

THIRTY-THREE

The Dacianos—Viktor, Stelian, Trehan, and Mirceo—were back in the court, awaiting the king and queen, and a lead that might help them find Mina. Days had passed without a sign of her. Even Balery couldn't get a read on her.

"You need to drink, nephew." Viktor sat on the edge of the throne dais, using a blade to clean his claws. "Or you'll never heal."

Mirceo limped as he paced back and forth across the court. He hadn't had a drop of blood since learning of Mina's disappearance. No intake meant Mirceo was slow to regenerate from Lothaire's beating the other day.

After Mirceo had demanded to know what the king had done, Lothaire had steepled his fingers, his black claws glinting. His deep voice had resonated as he'd said, "I sent Kosmina out into the world." He'd shrugged. "And damn if I haven't misplaced her."

Consumed with wrath, Mirceo had attacked the ancient vampire. Half-feral Lothaire had relished the opportunity to thrash someone, laughing as he'd broken Mirceo's bones.

It'd taken all of the Dacianos to pry Lothaire off of him. Mirceo's jaw had been so mangled he hadn't been able to tell anyone about his skirmish with the Forbearers, instead having to write out his suspicion: *Forbearers took her. Exchange for Kristoff.*

Lothaire had led the Dacianos in an incursion on that order's castle. Yet there'd been no sign of Mina. Fortunately Lothaire had an asset, a prisoner they could torture for information. Today they were supposed to learn the findings. . . .

Stelian swigged from his flask. "What is taking the red-eyed bastard so long?"

Though Mirceo wanted to murder Lothaire for sending Mina out, he berated himself just as much for not being here for her. He'd planned to talked to the king about keeping Mina close, but Mirceo had gotten so caught up in his own life that he'd let her down.

He'd lost the only things in his life that mattered, and in both instances, he'd deserved to.

Trehan checked his watch. "I'm due in Abaddon to meet Bettina. I must leave anon." He frowned at Mirceo's mottled face. "None of this need ever have happened."

Mirceo had been forced to come clean about the priceless crystal's end, and since he'd been viciously beaten, brain-bruised, and unable to lie, he'd unintentionally implicated Caspion.

"I could kill that demon for destroying the crystal," Trehan said, his piercing green eyes flickering black. "If not for him, Mina would be safe at home right now."

Mirceo didn't hate Caspion over the crystal, because he blamed himself for that as well. He'd pursued his mate so aggressively that the demon had snapped.

And for what?

Mirceo wished he could tell Caspion that his morning-after

panic had had nothing to do with their relationship and everything to do with Mina. He was convinced his arm pained him because she had been likewise injured.

When he'd explained his confounding reaction to his uncles, Trehan had said, "The night my Bride was attacked by Vrekeners, I woke from a dead sleep, feeling as if I'd left something undone." Mirceo had felt like a secret danced just out of reach. "That sense was maddening, because I'd always done what was expected of me. Always. Soon it grew into abject dread. I later realized that we Dacians have vaster abilities than even we know. . . ."

Damn it, how much longer would Lothaire be?

Reaching into his pocket, Mirceo ran his fingertips over Mina's last letter to him, one that'd gone unnoticed on his desk until *after* he'd discovered her missing.

He'd long since memorized the words, the parchment stained from his blood tears:

My dear Mirceo,

I have such exciting news! I'm being sent out into the world, as an official observer for King Lothaire. I know you expressed concerns, but I dare not disobey an order from our regent!

I am beside myself with anticipation, and can't wait to behold the otherlanders' world—the splendor of its natural beauty and the nobility of its peoples.

Brother, my heart soars.

Please don't worry about me as I set off on my mission. Such a request should prove next to impossible for my protective big brother, but try.

Your little sister is actually quite capable.

I have you to thank for that, for everything. Whatever would I do without my Mirceo?

I love you more than diamond-filtered sun,
    Mina D

Her words had rained down more blows onto Mirceo's already battered conscience. He should have taken time out of his busy schedule—being a fucking *degenerate princeling*—to escort her out into the world and teach her about it.

The degree of her innocence would likely get her killed. If other immortals or the plague didn't annihilate her, then the mortals would.

This letter might be the last communication he ever had from her. She could already be . . . dead—

Lothaire and Elizabeth finally arrived, teleporting into their thrones.

Moments later, two burly guards appeared with a shackled and gagged Kristoff. Blood and bruises covered the Forbearer king's face and bared chest. The guards had to hold him upright.

He looks even worse than I do.

"This one hasn't surrendered to torture," Lothaire told the court. "Understandable, since he shares my blood."

Kristoff's clear eyes flooded black with rage, promising revenge.

Lothaire turned to Mirceo. "You will drink my brother and harvest his memories to discover where they are hiding Kosmina."

"Drink him?" The thought of piercing that male's flesh made Mirceo nauseated again.

Whenever he'd passed out for a few moments, he'd continued to experience Caspion's memories of hunts and adventures. With each one, Mirceo had fallen more and more in love with the bold, stalwart demon.

How could he pollute those memories with this strange male's?

Plus Mirceo had given his word to Caspion that he'd keep his dick in his pants and his fangs in his mouth. Biting Kristoff meant putting Caspion out of reach forever.

But to save Mina . . . Tormented, Mirceo traced beside the prisoner, all but pleading to Kristoff, "If I drink you, I will harvest *all* of your memories—so just tell me what we want to know and save us the trouble."

The gagged Forbearer king thrashed against the guards, a killing look in his eyes. He'd never cooperate.

Mirceo steeled himself. *For Mina.* Fangs bared, he leaned in. . . .

THIRTY-FOUR

C as traced to Bettina's chambers, finding her biting her nails and staring off into space.

Her eyes went wide at his appearance. "Cas! What happened between you and Mirceo?"

"It's difficult to explain. Where is Trehan? I need to speak with him immediately."

"I expect him any moment. But I don't think it's a good idea for you to be here when he shows."

Cas held up the poster. "Kosmina's truly missing?"

Bettina nodded. "Lothaire sent her from the kingdom—without Mirceo knowing."

Cas's claws elongated. "She's my sister-by-fate!"

Gaze glinting, she said, "I know, Cas. I'm so sorry."

He folded the parchment, returning it to his coat. "Mirceo must be going insane." Cas's mate had *needed* him that morning, and every moment since. He would never forget the pain in those gray eyes, Mirceo's plea: *Help me. Because I think . . . I think I'm losing my mind.*

Yet Cas's own insecurities had colored how he'd interpreted the vampire's reaction. Mirceo's words from another time echoed in his head: *Perhaps you don't lack faith in* me. *Perhaps you lack faith in* you.

Cas had assumed Mirceo wanted away from him, never considering another explanation for the young male's bewilderment.

Bettina said, "He's not doing well."

"You have no idea how protective he is of Mina. He raised her from when she was just a little girl. He even sensed she was in danger."

"Trehan sensed my attack as it happened. I think Dacians possess a tiny bit of precognition."

How could I have been so bloody stupid? The idea of Mirceo in pain, vulnerable . . . "Damn it, Tina, where is your husband? I must reach the Realm of Blood and Mist."

She tentatively touched his arm. "Cas, Trehan probably won't take you. He blames Mina's continued plight on you."

"Me?" Cas stared at her. *Oh.* "Because I destroyed the scry crystal."

She nodded. "He pressured Mirceo to explain what happened to it. And since vampires can't lie, the truth came out."

Cas paced her chambers. "We don't need the crystal. *I* will find her. The Forbearers likely took her." After they'd failed with Mirceo . . .

"That was the working theory," Bettina said. "But when the Dacianos launched an offensive on the Forbearer castle, they didn't find her. And their seer can't even scry Mina's general vicinity."

Cas frowned. "That bone roller would've been able to see Mina if the Forbearers had taken her." Then who—? Cas stopped short. There was an entity that eluded seers . . . one that might have interest in a female vampire.

The Gaolers.

They didn't just harvest criminals. They collected any threat to the Lore, including sick vampires. If Mina had been gone this long, she had to have left her mist, growing corporeal. Which meant she'd been vulnerable to otherland dangers.

Like the plague.

Cas had brought those collectors down upon New Orleans, the same place Mina had last been seen!

Trehan materialized into the room. All cool arrogance, he leveled his green eyes at Cas. "Precisely the demon I wanted to see."

Cas's muscles tensed, his chest bowing.

"I'd considered you a misguided whelp but not inherently flawed—until you committed such an idiotic act. If not for your reckless stupidity with the crystal, my niece would be safe in her home right now, instead of lost in a world she is woefully ignorant about."

At best. And Cas had had the nerve to bust Mirceo's ass for rashness? "You're going to take me to Dacia."

"You have no right to go there."

Horns straightening with fury, Cas said, "My mate's there. I have every right!"

"Yet you've been separated from him during the most painful trial he's ever known?"

Cas's gut clenched. "Are we going to do this again, leech? I'm much stronger than I was last time." For centuries, the need for revenge against this male had shaped Cas. Finally they would finish what had been started so long ago!

Bettina hastily said, "Trey, he'll go demonic to reach his mate—and he's five hundred years older than he was before."

Trehan wasn't concerned whatsoever. "Presumably with

hundreds more deaths under his belt? Then the whelp might present a modicum of challenge this time."

Cas bared his fangs. "*Thousands* of deaths. And I'll add yours to the list if you don't take me to Mirceo."

"Please, you two!" Bettina cried. "I'm asking you not to do this."

Now that he and Trehan were more evenly matched, a battle could last for hours. Days even. Cas burned to make him pay for that beating—but he burned even more hotly to protect his mate and his sister-by-fate.

Cas *had* paid dearly for his years of wisdom and discipline. Though he'd used neither when dealing with Mirceo before, he would endeavor to do so now.

Bile rose in his throat. "Damn it, we don't have time for this." *Only one move left to me.* Cas bit out: "I am asking for your . . . help. Please, vampire. Trace me to my mate."

Bettina gaped at him, and even Trehan looked taken aback. Both would know how difficult saying that had been for Cas.

Two weeks ago, those words would have been impossible.

He gritted his teeth, prepared for Trehan to heap on more humiliation. Though Cas hadn't begged for anything since he'd been a pup, he would to reach Mirceo. His damaged pride, his searing disgrace, his need for vengeance—none of that mattered in the face of his family's wellbeing.

"My gods," Trehan said with a look of wonder, "you must love the hell out of my nephew."

Cas gave a curt nod.

Bettina nibbled her bottom lip. "Please, Trey."

As Trehan gazed at his wife, emotion made his eyes flicker black. "You know I can deny you nothing, *draga mea*." He turned to Cas. "Very well."

Huh? "Just like that?"

"The past is done. Besides, without the scry crystal, we are in sore need of a skilled tracker."

Bettina ran to her husband's side. In a breathless voice, she said, "Thank you, Trey!"

The vampire grasped her hands. "I will take Caspion now, but I ask that you remain here. Things are volatile in the Dacian court."

She hesitated. "Okay. *This* time."

"I shall return soon." He pressed a gentle kiss to her palm that made her face flush. "Await me?" he asked, somehow imbuing those two words with layers of carnality.

She breathlessly nodded.

Releasing her with reluctance, he grasped Cas's elbow. "I must warn you. Mirceo's appearance is much changed." He teleported them into Dacia's court, off to one side of the immense and echoing room.

Cas caught sight of Mirceo, and his chest constricted. His mate's skin held a deathly pallor, bruises marked his face, and his clothes billowed on his wasted frame. He looked as if he would crumble under the weight of gravity at any second.

Standing beside a shackled and gagged prisoner, Mirceo gazed up at Lothaire—the red-eyed king—with a defeated expression.

What was happening? The tension between them was so taut it seemed to reverberate. *Figure it out later.* Cas readied to trace—

Trehan clamped his shoulder to prevent him. "Lothaire has been in rare form these last few days," he said in a low tone. "If you'd like to survive this day, I suggest you stay out of his way."

Cas growled, "Who hurt my mate? Was it Lothaire?"

"If the king thrashes you, how well will you be able to help Kosmina? You choked back your fury earlier with me. You must again. You have a family to think about now."

Cas sank his claws into his palms, grappling not to attack the king.

Lothaire stalked closer to Mirceo. "Do it. Do it for your sister," he said. "That is a royal command."

Do what???

Appearing dazed, Mirceo leaned toward the restrained male—toward his neck.

Cas's mate was about to bite another! He tensed to fling himself away from Trehan.

Just before Mirceo's lips made contact, a blood tear tracked down his cheek. He drew back, shaking his head. "I-I can't."

Cas *knew* how much Mirceo loved his sister, could see how starved the vampire was—how could he not bite that male?

Lothaire snapped, "If you don't drink Kristoff, I will."

"No way," the queen—Elizabeth?—said from her throne. "Any more memories'll send you right over the edge."

Lothaire gruffly said, "I'll be fine, Lizvetta. When did everyone get so fucking persnickety over this?"

"Forget it, Leo."

Lothaire turned to Mirceo, baring his fangs. "Kosmina is in jeopardy."

Another vampire male said, "Because you sent her out!"

"Do I need to crush your skull again, Viktor?"

A hulking Dacian with a flask in hand—must be Stelian—said, "As if you care about Mina. Let's not pretend."

"Kosmina Daciano is my blood relation. Mine. No one takes from me." To Mirceo, Lothaire said, "Bite Kristoff's godsdamned neck! Your sister's *life* is on the line."

"I know that!" Mirceo all but sobbed. "This is killing me!"

His pain is my pain.

Trehan increased the pressure on Caspion's shoulder.

Lothaire thundered, "Do it now! Do you not want your sister saved?" Abruptly changing tack, he softly queried, "Do you think she's *frightened* right now? Will little Kosmina *cry* for you? Don't you believe she's already injured?"

Blood tears streaming, Mirceo bashed his fists against his head.

THIRTY-FIVE

Mirceo beat his skull and tore at his hair. *Was* Mina crying for her big brother? Was she scared? *Is she . . . dead?*

Though the need to save her clawed at his throat, his fangs were dull and useless. His mind understood why this act was necessary, yet his body remained irrevocably faithful to his mate. Mirceo had even tried to imagine he was about to sink his fangs into one of Caspion's warm, welcoming veins, but his body hadn't been fooled.

He'd just thought, *I need my demon*, when familiar hands seized his wrists. A low voice soothed: "Hey, hey, love. I've got you." Strong arms enfolded him. "*Shh, shh.* Stop this, vampire. I've got you."

Caspion. Mirceo shuddered from relief. "Am I dreaming you?"

"I'm here."

Lothaire demanded, "Who the hell is this demon in my court?"

Pride ringing in his tone, Caspion said, "I'm the tracker who's going to get Mina back."

How had Caspion found out? How had the demon reached this kingdom?

Anger disappearing as if it had never been, Lothaire returned to his throne. "Continue, demon tracker."

"If she wasn't in the Forbearers' stronghold, then they don't have her. You waste your time. That's not the trail."

"Then who does have her? What *is* the trail?"

Caspion asked Mirceo, "Does your arm still pain you?"

"Yes. I believe she was injured, and I feel it. Have for days."

Caspion nodded. "As long as you feel that pain, you know she's alive."

"But where?"

"Why would an immortal vampire, a female, not heal from a mere arm injury?"

Realization. His legs gave out, and he sagged against Caspion.

"No, Mirceo," the demon murmured. "We *will* find her. And we *will* heal her."

Lothaire canted his head. "You think she has the plague. Interesting."

Interesting??? Mirceo almost attacked again.

Caspion said, "The Gaolers might have taken her to their dimension. Which would explain why your oracle can't see her."

"Ah, the demigod devils are riding again? They used to be much more active. Of course, there used to be many more sick vampires before those sweeps began." To the court, Lothaire said, "If Mina has the plague, then the Gaolers have her. Sadly, she will *not* be returning home."

"Leo!" the queen snapped. "You better start behaving yourself."

Mirceo nearly vomited again.

Lothaire said, "Those phantasms are untouchable—and there are few beings I consider beyond even *my* unholy reach. No one knows whence they come."

Caspion had said the Gaolers' dimension couldn't be reached. Dear gods, what if she ran afoul of Silt Harea—the male who'd threatened to kill anyone Mirceo loved?

Caspion squared his shoulders. "*I* can get to the Gaolers."

~

Lothaire laughed. "This I must hear. How can you find demigods?"

Cas said, "Because I know where they will go in the future— and when."

Mirceo cast him a questioning look.

Cas told Lothaire, "Mirceo and I are going to capture another one of their bounties. When the Gaolers come to collect, *we* will collect *them.*"

Lothaire flashed his fangs. The king's version of a smile? "I approve of your cunning. Which bounty will you retrieve?"

"There are several possibilities. Once Mirceo has fed and *healed*"—Cas directed a look of menace at Lothaire—"he and I will assess the bounties with other seasoned hunters."

"Keep me informed." Lothaire's attention fell to his gagged and shackled prisoner. "Apologies, Kristoff. Apparently your faction had nothing to do with the Dacianos' troubles. No hard feelings, brother." Kristoff yelled behind his gag, thrashing. Unaffected, Lothaire said, "I assume we're still on for our match this afternoon. I will even move your chess pieces while your broken fingers heal. Best keep your eye *on your queen.*" Lothaire took Elizabeth's hand. About to trace her away, he paused to ask Mirceo, "Why is that demon still embracing you?"

Mirceo lifted his bruised chin. "He's my mate."

Lothaire's red eyes widened and blazed. "I don't care how valuable he is for us to use, I forbid such a union in my kingdom!" He slammed his free hand down on his throne's armrest, disintegrating it. "Not on my watch! If you want that male, I'll exile you."

Sounding crazed, Mirceo said, "Then my mate and I are going to live in a dismal cave and hunt Wendigos for the rest of our lives."

Cas shot him a side look. *Pardon?*

Mirceo muttered to him, "I realized I would rather that scenario with you than anything else without you."

The queen snatched her hand away from Lothaire and glared at him. "What the hell is wrong with this match, Leo?" The angrier she got, the thicker her country accent grew. "They clearly care about each other."

"Mirceo is my *blood*! And he dares to proclaim this male as his mate? Bringing this"—he gestured to Cas and Mirceo—"into *my* court?"

Cas clutched Mirceo's frail form against him. He'd figured they would get pushback somewhere or sometime—simply because they possessed two dicks between them—but he hadn't thought it would come from a three-millennia-old vampire.

Voice thrumming with fury, the queen told Lothaire, "You had better check yourself."

Lothaire threw his hands up as if all the world had gone mad. "When Trehan mated a sorceress with demon blood, I tolerated the match, even encouraged it. But now Mirceo's mate is a *full-blooded* demon? With horns! Will Viktor bring home a Wendigo? Stelian will surely mate a ghouless. When we find Kosmina, she'll probably be knocked up with centaur foals. Lizvetta, there's only so much I can STAND!"

"Wait," Cas said, "you don't care that I'm male?"

Lothaire blinked those creepy eyes. "Why the fuck would I care if you're male?"

Then solely because I'm a demon?

The queen frowned. "For lordy sakes, I thought you'd be more tolerant since your queen was a human 'peasant' before you turned her into a vampire."

Lothaire gazed down into her eyes, and his expression softened. "Ah, but you were *different*, my love. There is uncommon greatness in you."

Her eyes went soft as well, and she gave a resigned sigh. "You're digging yourself deeper than a mole." She turned to Cas. "I'm Ellie, and I'm so happy to welcome you here to Dacia, Prince Caspion. I know you will protect Mirceo to the death and help bring back Mina. We officially recognize your union in front of all." To Lothaire, she pointedly said, "Don't we, Leo?"

Lothaire sneered to Cas, "We recognize this union." With a sinister grin, the king added, "We also recognize that the demon probably won't make it out of his upcoming mission alive. . . ."

THIRTY-SIX

Caspion drew Mirceo even closer, teleporting them to their villa.

"I have to be imagining this." Mirceo was so weakened that his vision had blurred, his thoughts a snarl.

"I'm here." The demon swept the backs of his fingers over Mirceo's cheek to brush away a tear. "I will be as long as you let me."

"You and Mina are the only things that matter to me. But I lost you both."

"You've lost *neither*." He cupped Mirceo's face. "Heed my words: We are going to find Mina alive. I took her poster from the board, entering myself and my partner into that contract. Together he and I have never failed to claim a bounty."

"You truly believe we can?"

"Yes. And when we bring her back here, perhaps Lothaire will view my presence as something other than an insult."

Mirceo trusted Caspion. If the demon said they'd find Mina

alive, then they would. The fears that had threatened to undo him began to recede to a manageable level.

"We'll leave as soon as you're ready. So you need to drink, leechling. You're far too young to go without blood."

"You're not the latest in a long line," Mirceo blurted out. "You're the last. My last. My ever. I need you to know that I kept my fangs in my pants and my dick in my mouth."

Caspion's blond brows rose. "Okay, vampire, you *really* have to drink now."

Mirceo frowned. "Am I making sense? Can't seem to think."

"We'll talk about all this once you've recovered. Please feed."

Mirceo swayed against him. "I might not keep it down."

"You will, because your panic will be less. You've identified the cause of it, and we know what we face. You understand the road ahead, and you better believe we'll prevail. But you need to drink to be strong for the job." Caspion drew a claw over the side of his neck, then cupped the back of Mirceo's head to press him to the bleeding slash.

Warm drops glistening against bronzed skin . . . Mirceo's fangs went razor-sharp, but he needed to get these words out. "Why are you being so kind to me after what I did? I fucked up that morning. And I fucked up months ago when I manipulated you. I am so sorry for that."

Caspion's brows drew together. "I can't regret what happened, because we're fated. But I'll kick your ass if you do something like that again. Now, *drink.*"

~

Though the vampire panted with starvation, he somehow dragged his haunted eyes away from the blood. "I need to know that we're bonded . . . that we will get back to where we were . . . the night you claimed me."

"No, leechling. Because I feel even more for you than I did then. I godsdamned love you." He thumped Mirceo on the ear. "Now, shut up and suck."

Mirceo gave a strained laugh. But he did ease closer and pressed his mouth against Cas's neck. Tentative licks followed.

"Bite, vampire."

With a weak growl, Mirceo sank his fangs into ready and waiting flesh.

"That's it, love." Cas gazed at the ceiling as he healed his mate, solidifying their connection again. "Drink."

As Mirceo sucked, his body began to fill out, his injuries mending.

"I'm strong for us," Cas assured him. "Take as much as you need."

Mirceo's reedy heartbeat slowed and deepened. Soon it had synced with Caspion's, one loud drum in their ears.

"You feel that, Mirceo?" He groaned in response, and together they basked in the connection. "You need someone to take care of you. Let me be that mate."

Mirceo's arms wrapped around Cas's chest, and he moaned his assent.

"I'm sorry that I didn't have faith in you," Cas said. "Or in my ability to keep you. I'll never doubt either of us again."

When Mirceo released his bite with a last lick, Cas's gaze roamed over his face. "There he is. There's my mate."

Mirceo's eyes had cleared, his gray irises brightening. Color tinged his cheeks, his lips reddening. "I can't believe you came back to Dacia for me. How did you get here?"

"Trehan traced me."

"Did you two fight?"

"I was desperate to get to you, couldn't spare the time. So I asked him very, very nicely to take me to my mate."

Mirceo raised his brows. "You must love the hell out of me."

"Trehan's thoughts exactly." Cas clamped his nape. "You're under my skin, Mirceo. When we parted, you took my heart with you. Go easy with it, okay?"

"I'll protect it forever, just as you'll protect mine."

"You saying you love me?"

"Madly. I already knew it the morning after, which is why I was so confounded by my panic." He gazed up at Cas, staring into his eyes. "We really are going to find Mina?"

"We'll storm hell if we have to." He took Mirceo's hand in his. *We fit.* "I will not let you down."

"What if Harea finds her?"

"Then he had better hope she can't lay hands on a sword. Somehow, someway, this family will best him a second time."

Mirceo gave a decisive nod. His expression grew focused and intent. "Then let's get started, old man."

Cas gazed down at the mate he loved. "You stay on me like my godsdamned shadow, vampire."

Mirceo's lips curved. "Eternally, demon."

WICKED ABYSS

Next up in the electrifying Immortals After Dark series.

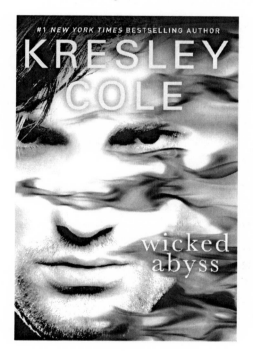

Coming April 25, 2017

This fairy tale doesn't end with a kiss . . .

A spellbinding Immortals After Dark tale from #1 *New York Times* bestselling author Kresley Cole!

The terrifying king of hell . . .

As a boy, Abyssian "Sian" Infernas had his heart shattered by a treacherous fey beauty who died before he could exact vengeance. Millennia later, a curse has transformed him into a demonic monster--just as she's been reincarnated. Sian captures the delicate but bold female, forcing her back to hell.

Meets his match.

Princess Calliope "Lila" Barbot's people have hated and feared Abyssian and his alliance of monsters for eons. When the beastly demon imprisons her in his mystical castle, vowing revenge for betrayals she can't remember, Lila makes her own vow: to bring down the wicked beast for good.

Can two adversaries share one happily-ever-after?

As Lila turns hell inside out, the all-powerful Sian finds himself defenseless against his feelings for her. In turn, Lila reluctantly responds to the beast's cleverness and gruff vulnerability. But when truths from a far distant past are revealed, can their tenuous bond withstand ages of deceit, a curse, and a looming supernatural war?

Read the extended bonus preview at:
www.kresleycole.com/wickedabyssexcerpt.pdf

CPSIA information can be obtained
at www.ICGtesting.com
Printed in the USA
LVOW11s1451170317
527609LV00002B/426/P

9 780997 215199